When Life Falls
It Falls
Upside
Down

Also by Lou Myers

A Psychiatric Glossary
Group Therapy
Absent and Accounted For

for children

Ha Ha Hyenas
In Plenty of Time
Tutti Frutti

When Life Falls It Falls Upside Down

◇　◇　◇

Lou Myers

Grove Weidenfeld

NEW YORK

Published by Grove Weidenfeld
A division of Wheatland Corporation
841 Broadway
New York, NY 10003-4793

Published in Canada by General Publishing Company, Ltd.

The following stories originally appeared in *The New Yorker* in
slightly different form: "The Old-Age Home," "A Summer with
No End," "Birdsong," "Too Good Is Unhealthy," "Live a Little,"
"A Midsummer Night's Dream," "Cousin Lillian," "Hortense,"
and "A Lazofsky."

Permission to use the short excerpt from *Juno and the Paycock* by Sean
O'Casey has been kindly granted by the publisher, Macmillan London.

Library of Congress Cataloging-in-Publication Data
Myers, Lou.
When life falls it falls upside down / Lou Myers. — 1st ed.
        p.   cm.
        I. Title.
        PS3563.Y434W47   1990
813'.54—dc20
                                            90-2701
                                            CIP

ISBN 0-8021-1177-7

Manufactured in the United States of America

Printed on acid-free paper

Designed by Irving Perkins Associates

First Edition 1990

1   3   5   7   9   10   8   6   4   2

To My Wife,
Bernice
With Affection.
My Thanks.

Contents

vii

When Life Falls
It Falls
Upside
Down

Too Good Is Unhealthy

◇

I
T WAS A HOT MORNING, and tenants were already seated around the stoop on folding chairs. Mrs. Klingman sat on the top step, one hand holding on to the iron frame of the glass door. She spotted me and Ma trying to leave the building. "Hello, gorgeous!" she called, reaching for Ma's arm and holding her—a signal for a chorus of "Hello, beautiful!" and "Hello, darling!" from the other women. I was driving Ma up to the Catskills for the summer. She said good-bye to her friends, kissing and promising to write and inviting them to come up for visits. People were going in and out of the building with dogs, and the street was covered with litter. When Ma shook hands with Mr. Glazer, a retired high-school teacher, he sarcastically asked how she could leave all this behind.

We drove to Ogden Avenue and picked up a friend of Ma's, a Mrs. Elkin, a woman in her late seventies, a few years younger than Ma. She was waiting for us in front of her house, surrounded by bundles, two satchels, and some pots and pans tied together with cord. Fortunately, I was driving a station wagon. Mrs. Elkin and Ma sat in the backseat, and as we drove off, Ma said, "Sara, this will be a special summer."

Our first stop was at a Goldberg's Dairy Farm—"We Have Five Thousand Chickens"—but they didn't have a casino or a social hall. We stopped next at Bronstein's Mountain House, in Woodridge: "Kitchen Privileges, Strictly Kosher, Rabbi on Premises, Lake Nearby." Bronstein's looked good to Ma, but on close inquiry Mrs. Elkin found out that the lake was at least a mile up the road, at Kaplan's Hotel.

"Sara," Ma said, "forget the lake. They've got cows in back, and that means milk straight from the cow to our table."

Mrs. Elkin wasn't convinced. "Straight from the cow," she repeated. "I didn't come up to the Catskills for cows."

So we drove over to Kaplan's Hotel. Kaplan's had rowing, golfing, swimming, and horseback riding but no *kuchalane* (cook yourself) facilities. We finally stopped off at the Chamber of Commerce booth in Monticello and I asked the man if he knew of a hotel for older people. He thought for a moment and then suggested Segal's Hilltop Hotel, which, he said, was a summer cottage for retired show-business people. "Wait a minute," he said, "I'll telephone Segal himself."

A few moments later an old man with one eye shut drove up in a battered Chevy, limped over, using a cane to steady himself, and introduced himself as Segal. Ma asked Segal if he had a private lake, and Mrs. Elkin wanted to know if his hotel was fireproof and if there was a casino. Segal said his place had twenty or so retired actors and entertainers from the Yiddish stage and that, yes, he had accommodations. "If you like the room," he said, "we can change the sheets and pillowcases and you can move in right away and beat the afternoon rush."

Ma laughed. "You hear what he said, Sara?"

Mrs. Elkin pursued the lake question: "Is the lake at your place or somewhere else?" She wanted to know if it had a beach, and did it have rocks and weeds, and did Segal replace burned-out light bulbs, and what about poison ivy? Segal said he took care of everything.

Ma wondered about Segal. Was he the same Segal, she asked, who made a recording of a Russian song many years ago—a barracks number called "Ertzym, Pertzym"? It was the one and only! Segal was thunderstruck that someone still remembered him. "It was on the Columbia label," he said, and then burst out singing in Russian in a cracked voice, half leaping about, flourishing his cane and finger whistling. Ma beamed at the greatness of Segal, who bowed in her direction and said, "Madame, the curtain is at last brought down, the audience leaves the theater, the splendor is over. . . ."

Ma was ready to go with him, and why not? Segal was living proof of pleasures to come. We followed his Chevy up a dirt road about a mile to a white frame house on top of a hill. A number of guests lay dozing on the lawn, stretched out on unmatched beach chairs. Segal said he would have liked us to meet his wife, the actress Ella Goldstein, but she was upstairs having her afternoon rest. "Ella," he confided, "entered the theater at the early age of twelve, playing the role of Anna in *Chanele, the Dressmaker.*" An old man lay snoring nearby in the shadow of an elm tree. Segal whispered that he was the great Joel

Epstein, famous for playing Chasidic rabbis: "Joel Epstein came on with a wild leap. He was all movement."

Ma remembered him from the old Grand Theatre. "Joel Epstein," she said. She leaned over the sleeping man. "I saw you in serious theater years ago, in Leibelle Wolf's *The Shochet's Knife*. In the first act, you came home from your job in the chicken market and found your wife, Rifke, in your best friend's arms. Such acting. Such heartache."

Joel Epstein opened his eyes and said, "Applause and bravos so far from my public, so far from my dressing room. . . . You are too young, madame, to remember."

Segal pointed to a man with greenish-white hair, sleeping with a newspaper over his face. "And here is Halpern, the tenor. His rich voice could scarcely be matched. Over there is Merle Effrom, from *Good-bye, Becky Cohn*. She looks good in spite of the years."

Ma had great expectations. There would be conversation and show biz. But Mrs. Elkin didn't believe a word of it and wouldn't get out of the car. "They're having a sleeping contest up here!" she muttered.

The following Saturday I drove Ma and Mrs. Elkin up to Hurleyville, in the Catskills, to a Shapiro's Farm, a ramshackle cottage on a tilt over a gully with a pond at the bottom. They took a room there with a gas stove, an early-model refrigerator, a bread box, a small table, and a chair with loose legs. I warned Ma and Mrs. Elkin not to stand on the gully side of the room or the cottage might tumble into the pond.

Shapiro was a tall, erect, pink-cheeked man of seventy-five, still robust. He asked 140 dollars for the season, and Mrs. Elkin offered 100. Shapiro declared, "All of us together here revives memories of my childhood, my old friends, the houses, the streets. . . . I'll let it go for one hundred and thirty." Ma offered 110, and they all settled on 120. Shapiro then produced a contract with four duplicates: one for himself, one for Ma, one for Mrs. Elkin, and one if the others got lost.

"Don't worry," Shapiro assured me, "your mother will be among friends. God forbid, if she needs a doctor, we are five minutes from the village. And God willing, your mother will enjoy the best of health and come back next year."

Ma raised her eyebrows and said, "Health is better than money."

Mrs. Elkin wasn't convinced. "Too good is unhealthy. We're not as young as we used to be."

A few days later Ma telephoned me to say that she and Mrs. Elkin had had a falling-out. Mrs. Elkin had rented a TV set and had it placed on the table against the wall near the bathroom. The door had to be opened carefully or the doorknob would hit the TV screen. Ma turned on the set and sat down to watch. Mrs. Elkin came in and changed the program. Ma got mad and went into the bathroom. On her way out she ran the doorknob into the screen. "Later," she told me, "Sara loaded Shapiro up about me. She told him that I was ruining the stove and that I kept the light on in the bathroom all night. Shapiro, with a thirst for justice, comes into our room the next morning. We weren't even out of bed yet. 'Mr. Shapiro,' I told him, 'there is no greater honor than to knock on a door before entering.' Shapiro said that houseguests and fish spoil on the third day. I told him that if one person tells him he has donkey's ears, forget it; if two people tell him, he should buy himself a saddle."

I asked Ma if she had finally worked it out with Mrs. Elkin.

"After breakfast we made up. She said to me, 'It all goes in one ear and out the other.' 'Darling,' I told her, 'the ears don't know what the mouth says.' "

I went up to Shapiro's the following Saturday and joined Ma on the lawn. Ma, being walleyed and hard of hearing, floated out among the other guests with great delicacy, almost on tiptoe, to offend no one. She introduced me to a Mr. Greenberg, who sat under a sun umbrella. Mr. Greenberg was especially kind. "Sit down," he said to Ma. "Help yourself to a tangerine."

Ma telephoned me a week later to say that she had stayed under Greenberg's sun umbrella a little each day. On the seventh day, he erupted in anger at her for reading his newspaper. The Greenberg who always said "Sit down, Drezzle, and don't be strange," roared, "What should I read—the wall?" Ma dropped the newspaper and stood up in a panic. Greenberg's bellow had brought the others up from their beach chairs, their heads turned in Ma's direction.

"I told him," she said to me, " 'Mr. Greenberg, I defy you and your base instincts. You're not dealing with the weakling you're expecting to terrorize. I'm nobody's fool.' "

"You said that to him, Ma?"

"Not yet. It takes time."

I went up to Shapiro's Farm again the following week-end. After lunch Ma and I went out on the lawn to sunbathe, and Mr. Greenberg was there, talking passionately to Mrs. Elkin and some other women. He took a radical turn, winding himself up in a Lenin suit, sliding into dialectics. "Water when frozen," he said, "turns into something called ice. And water when boiled turns into steam. These are quantity-quality changes, and it's the same with people."

Ma caught him on his dialectics. She ridiculed the notion of changing people by boiling them. "It's the same with people?" Ma repeated. "When you boil a chicken, it's still a chicken, Mr. Greenberg. If your chicken turns to steam, you didn't watch the fire." The women thought Ma was very witty—so much so that Shapiro asked her to recite part of a play by Chekhov in the casino that night.

It wasn't easy for her, but dressed up in pink with a flower in her hair, she fixed her good eye on the page and read with so much feeling that the audience of old people gave her tumultuous approval. Seeing this, Mrs. Elkin also came forward to read, but it wasn't the same thing. Ma was a hit!

Ma was now the center of attention at Shapiro's Farm, and though she had no conceit, her language flowered. The next morning, as we walked out onto the veranda, we met Mr. Greenberg, and Ma greeted him: "Dear friend, may you have long years. May you have health, luck, and happiness. May you fall down and break your neck." The remarkable nobility of Ma's new appearance was not diminished by her age. She had words of good health and praise for everyone, and the opening of a newspaper, the putting on or off of a hat, the mere adjusting of her eyeglasses was not so small a thing as to be done without a certain manner.

It was raining the next time I came up to visit Ma. We joined the guests in the casino to wait for the weather to change.

"You see, Leon, the sun shines brighter after the rain," Ma said.

Mrs. Elkin sat down next to Ma. "If everybody says so, it must be true."

Shapiro, behind the bar, poured everyone a glass of wine and toasted the group: "Your good health and peace."

"Nobody can make you cry like Shapiro," Ma said, in tears, as Shapiro sang, accompanying himself on mandolin: "Do I really see you, my little town, or is this just a dream?" When he finished, he asked Ma to do a reading. Ma hurried back to her room and returned with a book by Sholem Aleichem.

" 'A clumsy wagon drawn by a dispirited nag crawls along the narrow path which leads from the city of Boiberik to the village of Anatevka. . . .' " Ma's declamation had improved considerably. She paused and looked away from the page from time to time; occasionally she would smile or affect a frown.

She read in the casino two or three evenings a week for the rest of July. She told me that Shapiro said he had been fifty years in the business and had yet to meet her match.

I came up on the first Saturday in August to see Ma in *The Bigamist* at the casino. Admission was one dollar. Ma had one line in the half-hour epic, but it was only a two-character play, and she was onstage with Shapiro from the start. The stage was so small that they could hardly turn about. The curtain was pulled open by a Mrs. Katz, who also accompanied the show on violin. Shapiro sang, wept, and tore at his hair as he played Abrom, a man who betrays his wife, Dorapova, who has just died. Meanwhile, Abrom tells us, another woman, Merelle, has borne him a son and threatens to throw herself off a cliff unless he marries her. Abrom instead capriciously marries a third woman, Rifke, played by Ma, who has come into his life, though he still loves Dorapova, his first wife. Shapiro then sings a number of different character parts. Now he is the rabbi, instructing Abrom to put the ring on Ma's finger, and the next minute he's Abrom again, in remorse over Merelle. Ma, as Rifke, now speaks her only line: "Life is where it takes you."

A Mrs. Schindler told Ma that if it weren't for her, they would all have slept through the piece. Another woman said that Shapiro had a captive audience and that Ma had given *The Bigamist* a fresh look for a change.

On Labor Day I went up to Shapiro's Farm to bring Ma home. From the window in Ma's room I could see the hills and the small wooden bridge over Shapiro's brook. There were butterflies and breezes and country smells, daisies and black-eyed Susans quivering in the fields. A quarter of a mile down the road I could see Ma and Mrs. Elkin picking blackberries in a bramble patch.

By the following summer Shapiro had closed his farm and entered an old-age home. Mrs. Elkin was spending the summer in Arizona with her son, so I took Ma alone up to a Levinsky's Dairy Farm, in Kiamesha Lake. Levinsky had thirty cows and farmed all day, while his wife took in roomers. Within a week I got a telephone call. Ma was in agony. There was no one to speak with. She drifted about, trying to get into conversation. Perhaps she wasn't heard: she had grown more hard of hearing, and her voice might have come out in a croak. Her eyes were worse: she had the wandering gaze of a lobster. Poor Ma. She had been so successful only a year before, and now to be unable to pry one of the women cardplayers loose from a game . . .

"What the earth covers, the heart forgets," said Ma, back home in her apartment again.

I told her that if Shapiro were twenty years younger and had a ten-piece orchestra and a thirty-foot stage, he would still be around.

"Shapiro," said Ma. She shook her head. "He always made a terrific exit, but to go into an old-age home . . ."

The next day she found that her friend Mrs. Klingman was moving in with her sister in another neighborhood. Mrs. Diamond, from the apartment next door, was in the hospital, and there weren't many of Ma's friends left. There had been one particular pest, a Mrs. Klar, who for years came out of the most unlikely places to lean on Ma. "Drezzle, you're going up to the store anyway," she'd say, and give Ma a list of items to buy for her—the kind of person who lives forever. She was gone, too. Ma would have given anything to have her visit again.

"At least there used to be someone to talk to," Ma said over the telephone. I asked her about the bingo games in her apartment, and she said that Mrs. Tucker, from apartment 4-G, the last to play, had stopped coming in.

" 'I was, so they said, a child prodigy: I had quick wit, a logical mind, and a warm heart. . . .' " Ma liked to read from Isaac Leib Peretz but had been unable to find a group to recite to since Shapiro's Farm. I phoned Ma and asked her if she wanted to try it over at the Senior Citizens' Center on Southern Boulevard, in the East Bronx. Ma was glad to get out of the house, and she dressed up in a special gown of green chiffon, belted with a three-inch girdle of satin and a large buckle embroidered in lacquer red, dull blue, olive, and gold. Unfortunately, when we got there, we found that the center had been burned out some weeks before and was only a charred and gutted wreck.

"I should have telephoned first," I said as we turned around and drove back.

A few months later Ma began to see enormous gold bugs flying around the house, flashing on and off. Her landlord, Mr. Leibman, sent the exterminator to her place four times in one week and finally phoned me. "She's imagining things," he said. "After all, your mother is in her eighties, God bless. If we spray too much, it won't be safe for her."

On September 2, Ma's birthday, we drove out to the Fordham Diner. The car door on her side was stuck, so I tried to pull her over and out of the door on my side. She leaned toward me but hadn't the energy to lift her legs. I left her in the car and went to get her a sundae. On my return I found that she had slid onto the floor between the driver's seat and the steering wheel. I lifted her with a struggle, and she came up holding some carpeting. She smiled and said, " 'My memories fly and roam freely, singly and lightly, like particles of dust. . . .' "

At the end of November, Ma and I went down to the storage room to find her trunk. Mr. Coglan, who had been superintendent since the house was built fifty years before, pointed to a pile of folding chairs in the corner. "I knew them all," he said. "Diamond, Haggerty, Klar, Smith, Conti, Epstein . . . they were all here only yesterday. Right, Mrs. Mehler?"

"It was only yesterday," Ma said, looking at the chairs. "They were all busy flapping around, opening and closing, with old friends sitting in them."

My brother Ronald and I tied Ma's living-room carpet

to the top of his car. We were closing her apartment. There was no one outside to say good-bye to her as we drove away.

"One remembers everything at once," Ma said to no one in particular. "It's a holiday in the middle of the week."

Old Memories

◊

A RUNAWAY HORSE ran out of D'Amico's stable and fell down onto the railroad tracks on Park Avenue. The horse was both electrocuted by the third rail and shattered from the fall below. The uptown train stopped for an hour, as they had to get a derrick to hoist the dead beast off the tracks and onto the gutter. I worried about the third rail and about dying that day and could it happen to people. The things I remember. . . .

We were an immigrant family and had moved to 184 Street and Washington Avenue in the Bronx, in an Irish-American neighborhood. It didn't take my sister, brother, or me long to speak English well enough, but my father and mother spoke mostly Yiddish.

The O'Neal family lived on the ground floor front. Mr.

O'Neal was a chauffeur for a Westchester millionaire and had four sons; the youngest boy was my age and had a harelip and spoke funny . . . every other word that came out was "Yookaka." This one day I walked down the stoop just as "Yookaka" popped out of his house right in back of me. Stretching a rubber band as far as it would go from his eye to mine, he let go of the band and snapped the wrong end into his own eye. He shrieked, and his father, Mr. O'Neal, came out onto the stoop dressed in a black chauffeur's suit and slapped Yookaka a hard crack in the face. Pa looked down from our window and called, "Mr. O'Neal, you didn't hev to heet him so hod."

Mr. O'Neal shouted back: "Mind your own business!" Pa's accent was improving.

Mr. and Mrs. Kennedy, living on the fifth floor, were always drunk, and their twelve-year-old daughter had no family protection. She was a pushover for the gang outside and they all knew she "laid." It seemed hard to understand why some girls did and some didn't in 1924.

Some of the kids had a poetic flair:

> "Izzy, Ikey, Jakey, Sam,
>   We are the kids who eat no ham.
>   Football, baseball, swimming in the tank,
>   We're the boys who put money in the bank."

Jimmy Mulhall, the janitor's son, called me "Jewboy," and that was the first fight I had. I beat him up and Jimmy and I became fast friends.

★ ★ ★

A few days later my brother Ronald, while chopping wood in the lot, gave himself a splinter and cried out, "Jesus Christ!" Some of the kids, hearing him, gathered around and were on the verge of giving him a thrashing for his outburst. Mr. Mulhall came out of the cellar, and throwing his arms around Ronald, he shoved the kids loose. "Leave young Ronald alone. He'll soon be a landlord and you'll all be paying rent to him." We were in a new neighborhood.

I had to admit, Miss Smith, my kindergarten teacher, was a dream. At the least smile from her, waves of magic ran through me, her every movement was lovely. We all sang, "Oh, do you know the muffin man . . ." She sang in an undertone. Her singing wasn't loud at all; it was no more than a murmur. I still remember her. Pa went to Open School Week and came home laughing at my recitals: "Seesaw, seesaw, up and down, up and down . . ."

There was a sixteen-year-old girl, Cecile, pretty as a picture, who had jumped off the roof, and as she lay dying in the courtyard, the parish priest was praying over her. "It's a mortal sin to commit suicide," a neighborhood woman sighed. I stood around in a circle of people looking down at her. Her mother, Mrs. Laughlin, came out to see Cecile lying there. She let out terrible screams, her awful grief . . . Her hair hung loose, falling down over her eyes in gray wisps. . . . She threw herself in full length next to Cecile: "Tell me, my angel, why did you do it? . . . why did you do such an awful thing . . . tell me, my darling, my treasure . . ." The ambulance had come. I thought of death that day and many days after. Old memories stay with you the longest.

Yookaka showed up with a big rubber band on a forked stick, a kind of slingshot for shooting birds. "Let's practice," he said, "then we'll break a window. There's an easy one on a hundred and eighty-fifth street. . . ." OK, it seemed like a good idea, and we walk toward the corner. "We'll start here," he said. School was just out and the crowd would make a handy getaway. He passes me his slingshot. I put in a big stone. . . . I pull it way back as far as the rubber can stretch. "Watch this up there!" I say to Yookaka. And bam! Crash! Right into a window! I stand there like an idiot. People come running. I'm cornered. They start pulling at my ears. "William!" I cry out. Yookaka's melted into thin air! He's gone! At home the slaps rain down and fast. I can't see straight.

It seems that what I recall most about growing up was the street life of those days and particularly of my father and how he appeared to me. I remember climbing up this bluff in our neighborhood lot and somehow began to roll downhill. I tried to get a grip onto some nearby weeds but I rolled faster and faster, finally rolling over the cliff, crashing down onto the sidewalk. Pa saw me from our window and ran down, snatching me up in his arms, then running across 184 Street, turning left onto Washington Avenue, swinging into 187 Street, the Italian section, then straight ahead into Southern Boulevard, left again, and across Fordham Road, and right into Fordham Hospital. It took ten stitches to close the wound in the back of my head. Why didn't we take a taxi? There weren't many cabs in the Bronx in those days. Or telephones, for that matter, in our neighborhood in 1924. It was also Sunday and the drugstore on Park Avenue was closed. Pa did the best he could.

Pa bought us a Sonora record player and that was magic. A few weeks later he had his heart set on a Caruso record. We went to a music store in the neighborhood and Pa asked me to whistle "O Sole Mio" for the man in the shop. I became self-conscious and refused to whistle. Pa struggled with me, and by that time even if I had wanted to whistle, I had already forgotten how it went. Outside the store, Pa gave me a clout and a kick to make me shake a leg while crossing the street. When we got to the house I couldn't keep from crying. "You little bastard," Pa shouted, "I'll give you something to cry about!" He climbed up the stairs behind me and I rang the wrong doorbell. Mr. O'Neal looked out. . . .

I had Saint Vitus' dance that summer. I twitched and shook like mad. Pa got me some medicine which smelled of lavender. He poured some of the liquid into a tub full of water, then dipped me into the bath, but I slipped out of his arms, popping about while he tried to grab me. His patience ran thin and he squashed me to get a better grip. The soap slipped out of his hands and bounced under the tub and there were wild collisions. Pa was sopping wet and yelling as he ran around, dripping and muttering, to acquaint me with the pitfalls that lay in wait for me. Once dry and dressed he received me with open arms. He leaned close to get a good look at me, gazing affectionately. I'd never seen him so moved. . . . My brother

Ronald always had a dreamy look about him, sheep-eyed and half shut. Somehow Pa never cracked him one, although he did chase him around the table once or twice.

The police gave peddlers a hard time on the street in those days. Pa was arrested by a cop, and at his hearing in the station house, he told the sergeant at the desk that he had given the cop a five-dollar bill to let him go. Another peddler had told Pa that if he gave an arresting cop five dollars he'd have no trouble. The sergeant sent Pa downstairs to the jailhouse below and some policemen gave Pa a beating. He came home the next day with a black eye.

Pa was working again and everything we said or did became funny. We recited Humpty Dumpty in Yiddish and Pa did it in Polish. Ronald went to junior high and could recite it in French: "Je suis Humpty Dumpty . . ." My sister Marion did it in pig latin: "Umptyhay Umptyday . . ." and we couldn't control ourselves about "Polly put the kettle on . . ." Once Pa started laughing, a little thing like "Baa, baa, black sheep . . ." couldn't faze him. He was a born comedian. Ma felt ashamed but in the end she laughed too. It was good for her. Seesaw, seesaw, up and down . . .

I worried that the Brooklyn train might fall down with us into the street because there wasn't any catwalk along the tracks. . . . Ronald muttered, "Shelluck, shelluck . . ." imitating the sound of our train, adding "pshhh," each time the doors opened and closed. My uncle's old house was made of pink imitation bricks with small, staring windows in a row on the side street and a conical roof like a cocked Santa Claus hat on top of the house on the Myrtle Avenue side. They had a large tin sign painted in vivid yellow that swung to and fro in the passing breeze, COOPER'S DRY GOODS. We ran through the narrow door under the sign and into the hallway with the familiar smell of Vick's VapoRub. We rushed up the stairs. First we'd kiss my aunt, followed by a stampede for the frankfurters. We didn't peel the "specials" but bit into them skin and all to hear them pop. There was pastrami and corned beef and lots of Jewish rye bread, heaps of potato salad and an abundance of Dr. Brown's Celery tonic to wash everything down. My aunt then served the strawberry shortcake with cream soda, followed by ladyfingers with fudge ice cream. My aunt had six children, three boys and three girls. After we gorged ourselves, we all went into the far living room empty of furniture where we played handball against the wall.

On Washington Avenue I saw this cocky kid walking up on top of a billboard, his arms spread out, keeping his balance, and I called out, "Hey, kid, how'd you like a punch in the nose?" Well, he climbed down and beat me up pretty good. In the house Pa asked how I'd gotten my bruised face. I told him that this kid was bigger than me and by the time he came down after me it was too late not to fight him.

Pa sometimes took us to the Starlight Amusement Park near West Farms in the Bronx. This day I got lost in the Hundred Mirror Chamber with the bending floors. I tried to get out. First the many profiles then the back of my head lost! Ronald floated by in many reflections, solving his direction with the help of his pocket mirror. A dwarf in a clown suit took us through a door and we were outside again. We rode the Dew Drop and the Scream Machine. Ma didn't go on the Barrel of Fun after her tumble on the Human Pool Table. We stopped and shook hands with Zip the Geek and the world's tiniest midgets. None of us got on the loop-the-loop. Pa threw and hit some wooden milk bottles, knocking them over and winning a Kewpie doll for Marion. Ronald and I played the Penny Arcade and Pa had his Strength of Grip tested. Later we had soda and cotton candy.

Pa was up to his ears in debt. He had borrowed some money from my aunt without ever returning it. My uncle couldn't stand it . . . this couldn't go on. . . . "Even the suit he's wearing he doesn't own outright," he'd say to my mother. My uncle was all set to chew his ears off. Pa wouldn't even let them get started. He'd kiss my aunt and uncle each in turn as they came into our house. He was mighty glad to see them. He disposed of any sordid memories about money with a sweeping gesture. And the way he looked at my uncle, as if he were a poor, obstinate crackpot. They expected to find Pa all shriveled up and repentant, hiding under the bed, haunted by creditors and marshals, but instead Pa was in the best state of mind. He'd never felt better. He'd have all Ma and Pa's friends in stitches. They were crazy about him. They'd run over to listen to his antics. Pa was a tailor and was out of work half a year, but he had something up his sleeve for everyone. He'd make coats for the wives of friends . . . and all for nothing. Poor Ma had to keep a close eye on him.

Yookaka put a wagon together with the wheels from a baby carriage. He was the chauffeur sitting up front steering with a rope connected to the front wheels. No rubber tires were attached to any of them. I pushed the homemade wagon from behind. We mounted speed as I pushed and ran downhill on Snake Hill. The wagon wobbled and my left arm got a deep slice from one of the wheels. Yookaka and I ran into Weisenthal's drugstore, my arm dripping a trail of blood. . . . Mr. Weisenthal made a tourniquet on my arm and we waited for the ambulance to come for me. I had nine stitches put into my forearm.

I recall two things that bothered me that summer day. . . . Pa had given me a toy gun which sparkled in a variety of colors when the trigger was pulled. He had wanted to surprise Ma and Marion while we waited for them to come downstairs. I wouldn't give it up to Pa and we struggled for it in the street. Pa pulled it loose from me and gave it to Ronald, then popped me in the head. The other thing that bothered me was an article appearing in the *Bronx Home News*. It anticipated the end of the world that night. Something about a comet hitting the earth. We figured that if eight o'clock passed during the movie and nothing happened, then nothing was going to happen.

Birdsong

◇

URING THE EARLY MORNING of this lovely, sunny, and cheerful day in the summer of the year when the sky was bright and blue, Pa, my brother Ronald, and I were passing along a countrified section of the Bronx. In those days the area around Jerome Park Reservoir was mostly undeveloped. The streets were unpaved and the only thing passing by was the Jerome Avenue elevated train, while a distant firehouse stood at the end of the north end of the hill at Mosholu Parkway.

Pa loved singing birds . . . canaries, warblers, wrens, and birds that chirped. We set out this day, Pa, Ronald, and I, with a corrugated box, a stick, and bread crumbs in the hope a canary would fly under the box, peck at the crumbs, unlodge the stick while the box would drop over the unwary bird. But the reason we actually came was to explore this old, disused tunnel alongside the reservoir which I had discovered a few weeks before with my friend Jimmy Mulhall. Jimmy and I had been catching catfish in this underwater passageway, using an abandoned, rickety rowboat with a single oar. It had taken Jimmy and myself a number of hours to maneuver through the tunnel, six feet from top to bottom and ankle-deep in most places, which extended about a mile out into an open pond.

This one day, Ronald, Pa, and I climbed down into the mouth of the tunnel, where we found the beat-up rowboat with the one oar as though it had been waiting for us. Ronald and I climbed in, and Pa, after removing his shoes and socks, rolled up his trousers and pushed us off. There was a lot of decay and perforations in the stonework along the tunnel, and bursts of sunlight lighted our way as we went. I warned Pa to be careful of the bloodsuckers in the water that could attach themselves to his legs, and that they were poisonous. He scraped a couple of them loose and examined one of them. It was an expanding and contracting worm, rubbery and deep brown in color, with a sucker at each end. Pa said, "If the front doesn't get you, Leon, the back will." Pa was funny.

Ronald had recently finished reading *Les Misérables*. He shouted loudly: "The tunnel is tortuous, fissured, unpaved, crackling, interrupted by quagmires, broken by fantastic elbows, fetid, savage, wild, submerged in obscurity with scars on its pavements and gashes on its walls . . ." The echoes were deafening as each word came back again and again, careening and passing away into a final hoarse distant croak. We continued hollering until

Pa, who had brought his harmonica, played "Ramona" with one hand, shoving the boat with the other. It was the most lovely of sounds reverberating and echoing farther and farther away. We emerged from the crumbled end of the tunnel and into the sizable pond next to the reservoir, where some boys were swimming and splashing about in the nude. We pulled the boat up onto the grass, and Pa set up the corrugated box with the stick and the bread crumbs. Along the bank there were tadpoles, frogs, catfish, a variety of sunfish, and lots of dragonflies. Ronald said it was an inner jungle, tier upon tier of reeds and lions and tigers and parrots.

The day was very hot and Pa decided to go in for a dip. He edged along slowly, slowly, until the water was up to his waist. And then suddenly the water was over his head. Pa couldn't swim! I was eleven and I couldn't swim either. Ronald could dog-paddle a little. Pa came up for air several times and Ronald reached out and tried to save him. God, yes, how Ronald tried, but Pa was thrashing about and it was impossible. Ronald began to lose control of himself and was saved by another youth who pulled him out of the water. By the time he went back for Pa, Pa was gone. The boys from the other side of the pond were running over to us, and we called for help toward the distant firehouse. "Help . . . a man is drowning! . . ." We shouted again and again to the faraway firemen who seemed to respond by coming forward and then seemed to disappear. Where were they? We stood about waiting, standing, it seemed forever, looking toward the tiny firemen coming forward again, then vanishing altogether. It was the worst kind of time, hoping, expecting, and wishing that Pa would come up out of that dreadful tarn. Maybe the fish would help raise him. Would I ever see Pa again? Was that how Pa would die . . . into those fractured rocks underneath? Were the pits below of such extent and depth that he had been carried down into a bottomless hole?

There was a steady and gentle breeze now and the sun was shining so brightly. Someone grabbed my arm! My heart leaped for a second. It was dear Ronald. A man was running toward us from another direction. "Don't worry, kid, I'll bring your father up!" Taking off some clothes he dived into the pond. He kept diving again and again, trying, but he couldn't find Pa and I remembered feeling sorry for his failure. Fifteen minutes later there was a rush of firemen who had finally climbed over the last slope. There were five of them in a bedlam all around us as they quickly stripped and jumped into the pond. After what felt like an eternity, they pulled Pa out of the water, his eyes open and staring at me. The men tried artificial respiration. With each squeeze unbelievable volumes of water gushed from his nose and mouth, and after a half hour or so the firemen quit. Pa was dead.

The police took Ronald and me back to our neighborhood and a crowd gathered in the street around us. A newspaper reporter from the *Bronx Home News* was waiting for us. He asked to borrow a picture of Pa and promised to return it in a couple of days. My mother and my sister Marion were just coming home from shopping. They noticed all the tension and the people and police standing around in front of the house. Then they saw Ronald and me. "Where's your father?" Ma asked. "Pa drowned," I said.

That night Ma and Ronald went down to the Fordham Hospital morgue to identify him. On Sunday morning we returned to the morgue to reclaim the body for burial.

The room was narrow with a high ceiling, and on both sides there was a Gothic window of stained glass gleaming in yellows, blues, and crimsons. Pa was in an open wooden coffin, dressed in black with a white shirt and blue tie, and looking across at his head, I noticed that his brown hair was parted on the wrong side. A rabbi came in and Ronald and I repeated the Kaddish prayer for the dead, with the rabbi saying a few words in English: "What a good and bright world this would be if we did not lose our hearts to it but what a dark world if we did. . . ."

My rich aunt came over to our house after the funeral, remarking over and over again: "How does a grown family man step into a spoonful of water in the Bronx and drown in the middle of the day?" As if the middle of the day and the Bronx had anything to do with it. "A full-grown family man in the middle of the day goes to catch canaries?" We couldn't tell my aunt it had nothing to do with canaries.

The *Bronx Home News* featured Pa's photo on Sunday afternoon, and the front-page headline read, BRONX MAN DROWNS. There was no special news that day so Pa was the big story.

"Leon, money slipped through your father's fingers like sand," Ma said a week after Pa's funeral. "It was all the same with him as long as it went out fast. He goes and drowns, takes off and leaves me. That was his nature. A born gambler, he never brought home a full pay envelope. In perfect health in the morning, dead in the afternoon. He takes off. Good-bye, and that's that."

In the weeks after Pa died, I stayed up as late as I could, afraid of nightmares catching hold of me. We played bingo a lot. The first night we played, we found out that it eased our pain just to call the numbers in cadence:

"B–8."

"B–8."

"N–35."

"N–35."

Ronald had bingo. Then Ma, then me, then Marion. I reminded Ma that it was just three weeks since Pa had won ten dollars at punchboard and had taken us to Loew's Paradise for the movie and stage show. We had arrived just in time to see Oscar and his gold-and-silver organ rise on a turning column—around and around, bells ringing, canaries chirping, Oscar in a purple jacket, his long arms sweeping over the keys, buttons, and knobs.

A few weeks after Pa's death, some friends came for a visit. Mrs. Farinello, a dark, handsome woman from apartment 2-G, came over with a pot of macaroni. "I lit a candle for Max after Mass this morning," Mrs. Farinello said. Mr. and Mrs. Belkin, friends from around the corner on Honeywell Avenue, came in, and Mrs. Belkin kissed Ma and tried to cheer her up with neighborhood gossip. Uncle Harry arrived. He grabbed Marion, tossed her up in the air, and caught her, rubbed her face with his mustache, and shouted, "I'm a sea monster with eight legs and three eyes!"

Ma was crying again. "I sit here for hours and Max is never out of my mind," she said. "Sometimes I think I hear him calling in the next room. I don't want to live anymore."

Uncle Harry gave a sympathetic groan. "Drezzle," he said, "for dying you have plenty of time."

Mr. Petrucci, our latest boarder, an elderly man, came

and suggested we all play bingo. Ronald ran for the cards and buttons, and we seated ourselves around the large dining-room table. We played a penny a number, and soon Uncle Harry pretended great losses.

"Drezzle," he cried, "I've lost everything!" He flayed himself. He added up the sum again and again. He cross-checked it. How much did it actually come to? It came to more each time. He went for a pencil and began to add all over again. Uncle Harry was very funny. "I'll say this for Max," he told Ma, "win, lose, or draw, Max always left the card table with a smile on his lips and a wave of the hand."

I remembered a night Pa brought three men home to play poker. At first, he was giving cards and taking cards as politely as could be. Then things went wrong for Pa, and he began to speak sharply. They weren't playing for the fun of it. They shouted numbers at each other. Ma, my brother and sister, and I sat on chairs against the wall, afraid to breathe. Pa was pounding the table with both hands. He didn't have a cent left in front of him.

Uncle Harry shouted "Bingo!" and broke up laughing, pulling in the pennies on the table. "Max," he said, "was one of those fellows who could show two aces and a king and then, almost in the act of throwing the cards, palm the king and substitute a third ace. N–39."

"N–39," said Mr. Belkin. He picked up a rubber doll from the floor and squeezed it. It squeaked "Mama!" and the company laughed. My sister said, "That's Dottie Darling," and began to sniffle. The doll was her last birthday present from Pa. Mrs. Farinello put an arm around Marion and said that she once had a Diddums doll that said "Mama" and "La-la" when you moved the arms up and down. "We called him Little Happy," she said, "and we loved him dearly, and when we lost him we were heartbroken."

"Are we playing dolls or bingo?" said Uncle Harry. "G–64."

Ma told everybody about the time Pa disappeared for a few weeks. When he returned, Ma wouldn't let him in the door. He tried to get through a window from the fire escape. I saw his face staring at me through the glass. His lips were moving, but I couldn't hear the words. Ma had mended his suit in a hundred places, patching the lining in every shape and color. The suit was falling apart. The moths had eaten the sleeves. Pa was out of work that winter. We were eating less and less.

Mr. Belkin piled up his pennies. He winked at Ma and said, "Drezzle, since Shirley and I got married, I haven't looked at another woman. She was enough. I–16."

Everybody laughed except Ma. "I–16," said Mrs. Belkin. "I never knew real happiness until we got married, and then it was too late."

"Marriage is all right for people with children," said Uncle Harry. His laugh reminded me of Pa.

I remembered Pa's voice calling me from the elephant house in the Bronx Zoo—a sudden "Leon!" sent shivers down my back. The first week after Pa was dead, I had waited every night at the station, hoping that he would get off the seven o'clock train. One dream returned over and over: Pa had been seen in the neighborhood and then I ran into him. He was walking with a strange woman on Belmont Avenue. He looked different. His hair was dyed black and his eyebrows were off, replaced by a cosmetic line in an arch. There were hints of purple and violet under his skin, forming a tracery across his cheeks and nose. Seeing my astonishment, he reached out and shook hands with me. "Leon, I hope I haven't fallen in your esteem," he said. His eyes grew moist. "It was only yesterday, Leon, that I put a Tinkertoy in the mail for you." I chased after Pa and the woman, hiding behind ashcans and parked cars, through a maze of streets and alleyways. Shaking with panic, I wanted to jump out, to plant myself in front of Pa and make him come home again.

Mrs. Belkin poked me and said, "Leon, pay attention. N–42."

Uncle Harry recalled the time he and Pa were out of work, "busted and disgusted." They had gone to the racetrack with their last five dollars and had come home loaded with groceries. "Drezzle, do you remember the string of frankfurters around Max's neck?" Uncle Harry laughed until tears rolled out of his eyes. He slapped the table with his hand, bouncing the bingo buttons off his card. Pa had had racetrack fever that year. He had a new bookie. At one throw, Pa won two hundred dollars at Belmont. It went to his head, and he began raising his bets.

Mr. Petrucci shouted "Bingo!" and Ma got up to serve some tea. She came back from the kitchen crying, with a snapshot of Pa taken the year before at Coney Island.

Uncle Harry tried to cheer her up with a thought: "If we didn't have to eat, we'd all be rich." It didn't help. The tears poured down Ma's face, and Ronald suddenly wailed, "Pa's never coming home again!"

Uncle Harry said, "I've been an orphan since I was six years old."

Uncle Harry? An orphan since he was six?

"We were eight children in our family," he said. "One evening in that terrible winter—it was twenty below outside. We were shivering, dressed in every stitch of clothing we had, listening to the ice cracking on the walls. That night, my mother and father went out into the forest for firewood. We never saw them again."

We all gasped.

"How we cried that day and for a hundred days after," said Uncle Harry.

Mrs. Farinello's chin quivered as she spoke: "I lost my dear husband, Mike, a few short years ago, and I've been alone since." She opened her purse and brought out an old "In Memoriam" column from the daily newspaper. Slowly she read, "In treasured memory of my dear husband, Mike, who fell asleep June 16, 1922.

> "Not a day do I forget you, Mike.
> In my heart you are ever near
> Loved, remembered, longed for always
> Bringing many a silent tear."

She began to weep.

Mr. Belkin said that his grandmother had departed this world recently, as had his wife's cousin Libby: "She was fine in the morning, color in her cheeks."

Mr. Petrucci remembered his cousin Louis, and Louis's wife, Carmela: "Some women flower up after marriage. Like chandeliers, full of tinkling pieces and bulbs. In this case, it was Louis who blossomed and got better-looking every day. Carmela wore the pants, and Cousin Louis never left her side for five minutes. Louis's white hair curled and flowed in splendor, as if to say, 'I'm Louis, I'm not finished yet!' He died last year, gorgeous to see, like he was ready for a wedding."

Ma gathered in the bingo numbers and began a new round. "B–13," she called.

Mrs. Farinello echoed, "B–13," her face wet with tears.

"O–9."

"O–9," said Mr. Petrucci.

"Mr. Petrucci here," said Ma, "is seventy-five years old and has all his own teeth. He's a picture of health. He doesn't even wear eyeglasses and has a full head of hair. He's a doll of a man. G–44."

Uncle Harry agreed: "He's a prince of a man."

"G–44," said Mr. Belkin. "A gem of a person. He's got a golden heart."

Ma decided to tell a joke: "On a very hot day last summer, outside Epstein's Candy Store, an old man fainted away. People rushed to his side, calling, 'A man has fainted! Give him water! Give him water!' The old man raised his head and with great effort said to the bystanders, 'Could I have a malted instead, please?' "

We all laughed, and Uncle Harry said, "That's very funny, Drezzle, even if I heard it before."

That night I dreamed that Pa opened the front door and came into the living room. But the living room looked different—like the entrance to the Park Plaza Hotel, softly lighted, with a thousand gleams from brightly polished brass, good Windsor chairs, and chandeliers. Pa had a raccoon coat thrown over his shoulders and a soft black hat on his head. His suit was of black broadcloth, and a long gold watch chain was draped across his vest. There was absolute silence for a moment, broken by the faint barking of a dog in the distance. "Sea Biscuit!" Pa shouted. "At ten to one! Do you hear me? One thousand dollars, to be exact! In my pocket!" Dear Pa. All our friends and neighbors were waiting and stepped forward to welcome him home again. A luster came over the great room, and I was aware of a new sound—the combined singing of thousands of birds, the sound that makes the Bronx spring so lovely. I did not hear one above the others—all were blended in a wonderful harmony—but by very close listening, I seemed able to pick out individual birds. There were wrens and blackbirds and thrushes, hedge sparrows, warblers, starlings, and whippoorwills, and a hundred others, and their singing came in one sweet song of heavenly music.

We were even poorer after Pa died, and for a while it appeared Ma might have to send the three of us to the Hebrew orphanage. A Mr. Lazaravitch came to register us but we didn't go. We held onto the steam pipe and wailed, and he got tired and left. Ma had changed her mind anyhow. We moved soon into a tenement in an Italian-American neighborhood at East 180 Street, and life began to change for us. Ronald entered high school and Marion and I were in grade school. Ma cautioned me as I left for school. "Try to keep out of trouble. Don't go running around with hoodlums. Think of your mother. . . ." I promised to be well behaved, obedient, attentive, kind, never to lie, and especially never to steal, and to promise to study my English and math. I looked at Ma and she was trembling all over. We couldn't hold back our tears. I began to cry and then Marion started . . . Ronald's lips trembled.

Pa was gone and I felt I had grown small. I saw a photo of myself from a Brownie camera, and it appeared I had condensed. I was wearing knickers and everything about me was half-baked. I looked short-legged and had no neck to speak of, my eyes teared a lot, and I had to wear smoked eyeglasses. My nasal passages were blocked. My nose would bleed for no reason. I didn't want anything. I didn't take up much room, but I'd have liked to make myself even smaller. To apologize to somebody, anybody. But then the following year I grew four inches and my eyes were better. I had stretched out that summer.

My attention span during this period was limited and I was placed in a '4' class, a collection of exciting but slow students waiting to graduate and go to work. At the end of each term our class was photographed outside the school building. Angelina, a large girl who had had an illegitimate child the year before, stood in front of me, as none of the Italians would stand in back of her because she was *molochio*. Our teacher, Mrs. Loeser, ordered me to stand behind Angelina, but I refused. Mrs. Loeser warned that she would stop the Home Relief for our family if I didn't obey her. The boys carried on that since I was standing behind Angelina we must be in love . . . and "soon Angelina and Leon'll have babies together." Angelina had the giggles. . . . One of the boys imitated her voice: "Leon, oh, Leon darling, I can't stand it. Don't make me a kid!" The Italians had a fit. A number of boys in my class crayoned some graffiti in the boys' toilet about me being in love with Sophie and worse. Sophie on top and Sophie on bottom. Many of the students were two and three years older than I. Sophie was fourteen. She powdered and painted her face and wore an enormous hat with a bed of artificial daisies, a regular hanging garden. She walked behind me this day on the way out of school and some of the guys standing a few yards away were rocking with laughter. Sophie didn't appeal to me. In fact she gave me the willies. Passing an ashcan I saw a broken doll sticking out partly ripped loose with the arms hanging. I seized the doll by its torso and hit Sophie over the head, busting the doll apart. It all happened so fast. Sophie never stopped laughing, so innocent, so gentle, I even pulled her hair. For her it was love and laughs. Never had I seen eyes so full of happiness. . . . The Italians were in stitches. School was tough.

Sooner or later you had to find out who you could fight. I was about the sixth tallest in class. One day after lunch a guy by the name of Charlie came over and asked me who I thought I could beat up. I said, "Maybe Freddy." Freddy was an inch taller and huskier than I was. He was also a year older. Besides, it was only small talk, I thought. We hadn't gotten back to class from lunch yet when Freddy himself bounced over to ask me to fight him after school. I had a good chance to study Freddy and I began to worry. He delivered groceries after school and he had muscles which bulged all over. How did I ever pick Freddy? I told him I didn't want to fight him, and he said that sooner or later I would have to have it out with him. This went on for a month, with Freddy coming over to my desk every day asking me when we were going to fight. A bell rang for a fire drill and I laughed in line. Mrs. Loeser slapped me across the face and asked whether I was a Young Communist Leaguer.

A crowd of kids gathered after school to watch Freddy and me square off on the lot at Lafontaine Ave. A strange fight. Freddy had big shoulders. With his head lowered he charged, his fists moving back and forth on each side of me. At first I managed to hit him twice each time he came in at me. He never laid a fist on me, and after a while, instead of two blows I was hitting him three and four times and all landing on his face. My newfound friends were shouting for me to bring my blows into uppercuts. I gave Freddy a shellacking and after a bit he quit. Some of the kids saw Freddy leave with Mrs. Loeser, who had been waiting for him up the street. Freddy was out of school for a few days and came back at the beginning of the following week, his face still black and blue. We shook hands and Freddy had great respect for me when we'd meet. Mrs. Loeser never asked me if I was a Young Communist Leaguer again. I had come up in style. I was somebody; I wasn't tough, but I'd fight and that counted. It's hard to tell someone else how great it felt. I didn't have to stand behind Angelina and the guys didn't graffito my name in the boys' toilet anymore.

I was thinking of William S. Hart in *Tumbleweeds*. Pa liked William S. Hart's flat-brimmed Stetson and most of all his silent expression which showed a man of granite will.

Live a Little

◇

October 13

When I visit Ma today, she is dressed in a black velvet
skirt with big flares. Her white blouse is embroidered
with orange daisies. On our way out of her room, she
tells me she has joined the Women's Committee to Save
Lives—a group of residents of the Home who go around
the building to persuade the dying to fight harder and
continue to live.

"Nobody dies, Ma?"

"Better ten times sick than once dead," she says.

We meet a Mrs. Klein in the hallway. "Drezzle," she
says to Ma, "Abrams from Room four thirty-nine tried to
take his life yesterday. He dressed up in a full suit to throw
himself out of the window. He got stuck, and they picked

glass out of him all morning. Go up and talk to him. He's in a bad way in the infirmary."

Most of the Women's Committee to Save Lives are already in Isaac Abrams' room, sitting around his bed, rocking back and forth ever so slightly. Abrams, a large man, is even larger all bandaged up. Recognizing Ma, he fixes his eyes on her. Mrs. Adler, a woman in her seventies wearing a *sheitel*—a wig worn by some Orthodox Jewish women—drones from Hosea. "Come, and let us return unto the Lord: for he hath torn, and he will heal us; he hath smitten, and he will bind us up."

"I have no one left," Abrams says to Ma, "and now that my wife Hilda is gone, the shadow is on me."

Ma puts a hand on his arm and tells him that in killing himself he is killing her. Tears roll down her cheeks. "Isaac, we are all living under one roof."

Mrs. Adler touches his other arm and chants, "Isaac Abrams, we will never forget or forsake or cast you out of our presence, amen."

Abrams, somewhat astonished at all the attention, mutters, "A man here can never know whether he is in a home or a madhouse."

October 20
When I come to visit today, Ma tells me that Seligman, the director of the Home, was standing in the lobby at noontime—a chance for her to catch his ear. She told him that she'd been in the Home four months already and was troubled by the bronze plaque over each doorway, with a dedication to the late So-and-So who lived in such-and-such a room and contributed this-and-that sum. A memento mori, a constant reminder of the last mile. Ma noticed that Seligman was ignoring her, perhaps deliber-

ately. She then walked away slowly, to give him a chance
to call her back.

October 25
Ma is very busy in her new role. She thinks of herself and
the Women's Committee to Save Lives as "healers." Today when I visit with her, she takes me to Mrs. Malle's
room in the infirmary—the fifth floor. Mrs. Malle has
had surgery and is "recovering." She cries when she sees
Ma, and colored streams run down her face from her
makeup. Her room is spick-and-span, but there is a
smell, pungent and lingering. Once you catch it, you
smell it all the time.

Ma assures Mrs. Malle that she's on the verge of recovery and better times: "Tsipke, dear, you look better than
before you got sick."

We cross the infirmary to Room 509, where Max
Wilkins has been bedridden for the past month with a
broken hip. He tells Ma that in the Home a woman who is
still a girl at eighty is an old maid.

Ma laughs. "Max is a bachelor," she says.

Max responds, to me: "I knew your mother would
make it here the first time I saw her. After her first
appearance I remember saying to her, 'Drezzle, you've
got as much chance to get to Hollywood as I have.' Look
at me. How did I land in the Home? It was raining
outside."

October 30
A number of women from Ma's old fraternal branch of
the Workmen's Circle in the East Bronx join her to go up

and speak to Isaac Abrams, who has lost the will to live. They gather around Abrams, who is lying down in knickers and a red sweater, of all things. He has been crying, but on seeing me again, he checks his tears and tells me that if he wants to raise his right leg, it's his left that reacts. "I have a decayed body and a dying face," he says, starting to cry again.

A Mrs. Bloom chides him. "Isaac, what you did was stand yourself at the gate leading out of this world."

Ma shakes her head, saying, "Seventy-six years in this world and you can't wait to leave it. Life is a gift."

Abrams tells them that his life no longer makes sense. "I'm past all hope of recovery. The longer I live, the worse it is."

Mrs. Katz, a dynamic little woman, says, "One fool more or less in this world. There is no return match, Abrams."

Sally Stein, Abrams' social worker, pops her head into the room to say that Mr. Abrams is tired and ready for sleep, and we have to leave him to recover, more or less—to resume the life he led before. The women are slow to get up, and the social worker stage-whispers that Abrams has already lost one-third of his total body weight.

Abrams complains that he can't stand the sight of her. "That Stein, a person from three failed marriages and she gives me advice. I shake her out of one sleeve."

November 5
Seligman has agreed to see Ma. I go with her to his office. They face each other in silence. Seligman stares fixedly at her. His stare is already trying to dominate anything she

might say. Ma says that she's been trying to see him for weeks.

"In general," Seligman says, "interviews are neither deliberately accepted nor turned down. I must assume, Mrs. Mehler, that you know what this conversation will be about, and am therefore convinced that it would be to nobody's benefit if it actually took place."

November 12
We are on the fifth floor and drop in to see Abrams. The rest of the Women's Committee are already there. Seeing Ma and me, Abrams produces a bottle of port from under a pillow, opens it, and serves a little to each of us. With the first sip, gaiety overcomes the women. But just as suddenly sadness takes hold of them again, mingled with their pleasure, as their own happiness and miseries are remembered. They toast each other, and Ma salutes Abrams with "Isaac, may all your troubles be little ones." Their glasses clink. Mrs. Adler adds to the toast. "Here's to us all! God bless us every one!"

Ma says, "Isaac, we love you as a father and esteem you as a man of honor."

Sally Stein runs into the room and takes away the bottle of wine from Abrams, saying, "Mr. Abrams, aren't we a great favorite with the ladies." A general growl of disapproval rises from the women, who were only a moment ago nostalgic and sentimental.

"The doctors are worse," Abrams says. "They make things easy for themselves distributing sample pills. 'A discharge? Well, take some of these. Aching joints? Hemorrhoids? And how about your bowels?' Just as long as they've got some slop to put in your mouth and get you out of their office in a hurry . . ."

November 29

Abrams is talking to himself when Ma and I drop in. "I'm not with whom I want to be with, and then I don't know whom I want to be with. I don't want to be here. I want to be somewhere else. I want to be out there. I want to be where I am free again. I'm stripped of everything. I'm not what I used to be. I forget how to spell my name. I thought I was seventy-six, then counting the years backward I discovered that I'm eighty-two at least."

Last Tuesday, Abrams gave away his gold watch to Sam Hirsh, his friend from Room 410. That night Abrams swallowed a dozen one-inch nails. The doctor pumped his stomach and, after Abrams vomited a lot, got most of them out. I told Ma not to worry. "Chaz Chase, a vaudeville comic some years back, managed to eat everything from matchbooks to nails and broom handles." Ma wasn't amused. She feels that she's losing the battle with Abrams, that he is indeed bad news.

Down in the lobby, Seligman appears. Ma approaches him. "Mr. Seligman, isn't it possible to move Isaac Abrams downstairs to the first floor so that he can eat with his old friends in the main dining room?"

With lackluster eyes, Seligman looks down at Ma, saying, "Old friends in the main dining room? There are those here in the Home whose fury and resistance to all our efforts know no bounds and descend like an avalanche upon the heads of the already strained and exhausted nurses and social workers."

As we leave, Ma tells me she feels that Seligman is displeased with her, and worse. She says to me, "This morning I approached him about the possibility of moving Mr. Abrams to a room on the sunny side of the infirmary. He turned his back on me and then walked away without a by-your-leave."

December 4

Max Wilkins is still hospitalized, and we find him his usual exuberant self today. "I'm only staying here in the Home to try out new material which I can use later on Broadway," he says, "and when the season's over, I'll go home for a rest." We spend ten minutes with him, and as we leave, he says, "Don't forget to talk to Seligman about room and board for me for next summer."

Abrams is wasting away, and now seems tiny and bent in bed. He stopped eating voluntarily about a week ago. An Irish nurse is feeding rice pudding into his mouth and asking him to "embrace the greatness of its flavor." The nurse has tried every trick to get him to eat, and their battles have grown furious and exhausting for both of them. Dabbing her tears, she says that Abrams has been throwing chicken behind his chest of drawers and that last week the cleanup man moved the chest and found dozens of rotting pieces of chicken.

Mrs. Hester, in Room 515, looks like Voltaire, as do many of the others: very old. Mrs. Hester is in a bed with guardrails. She is playing with a rattle attached to an overhead cord. Like an infant she taps the rattle, and it goes up and down, and she taps it again.

December 14

Abrams is still at it. "I've lived out my time, and I've done my share of good and bad. Weeping and wailing will not be heard when I go. When I'm finished, I'll leave here in a whisper."

Ma tells Abrams he is an opera star—to get up and come down and eat in the regular dining room, four at a table.

He replies that he's sick of watching everything around him change. "Where is my wife, Hilda? She more than anyone understood me." Abrams' face is broken up. He seems on the brink of letting go all his pent-up sorrow until he notices me sitting up against the wall. "So," he says, "at her age, your mother—Drezzle—is invited to find a place here in the Home and begin life all over again."

December 23

Seligman is talking to Ma near his office off the lobby. "These are dark hours here in the Home, of course, such as come to everybody, in which people think they've achieved nothing in a lifetime at all. Where everything seems doomed to failure and then suddenly it starts to straighten out in spite of itself—without outside inter-ference."

At one o'clock I follow Ma up to the infirmary dining room, on the fifth floor, where she feeds lunch to an old friend, Mrs. Alcorn. Mrs. Alcorn, a palsied woman with fixed blue eyes, says "Hook" when she recognizes Ma. Ma tears pieces of white bread and dips them into the yolk of a soft-boiled egg. She pops them into Mrs. Alcorn's mouth. Ma is very patient as she feeds Mrs. Alcorn the rice pudding. She holds the spoon in midair, waiting for Mrs. Alcorn to open her tightly compressed lips. Ma keeps a steady drone going. "Eat, Sophie, it's good for you."

January 7

Ma won't give up on Abrams. "At least first write good-bye letters to your friends here in the Home. . . . Don't hurry to become nothing. . . . What is alive? . . . Dead you think you're a hero?"

Abrams tries to change the subject. "So this is your son," he says, pointing at me.

Ma is relentless. "Life is a gift," she warns.

Abrams complains that yesterday his social worker bounced in, whined, and held him tight, telling him to throw himself into life again. "Her despair reeks of cheese. I wanted to give her a good kick in the ass—" He stopped and burst out laughing. "Drezzle, you here for a visit? Why can't you leave me alone? What have I done to deserve this?" He is in tears again.

An old woman in a wheelchair reaches out and grabs my wrist as I pass with Ma. Her arm is noodle-thin, and I am afraid to pull loose from her, for fear of tearing it out of its socket. I am surprised at the strength of her grip as I unfold one finger at a time.

Ma says, "Mrs. Levy, you're gaining weight, and you will soon be up and around—maybe even go outside in the sunshine again."

I add to Ma's rhetoric. "And maybe even dressed in tights and running shoes, jogging up to Boston Road and back."

As we leave, Ma scowls at me. "What was that?" she asks. "You're not so clever, Leon. Mrs. Levy knows what's going on around her. It's just that the poor dear has lost her possibility as a total person. She certainly knows a dummy when she sees one."

January 15

The women drone Abrams a headful. "In the world, the way it is, one cannot be enough afraid to live. . . . It's not the stock-market crash. Take yourself in hand. . . . You must be dragged from your black thoughts. . . . Do you want them to say, 'Why him?' . . . In the afternoon you retire to death without self-pity. . . . What is alive? . . . All life is a dream. . . . Don't hurry to become nothing. . . ." Mrs. Adler reminds us of Isaiah, chapter 32. " 'And a man shall be as a hiding place from the wind, and a covert from the tempest; as rivers of water in a dry place.' "

Abrams says, "I turn my back on yesterday. I am beyond your reach. I am at an end."

Max Wilkins has his nurse in stitches as Ma and I come in. He is telling her about his father, who was always banging his head on something. "At least twice a day. My mother and my aunt knew he would get angry if they laughed in his face, so they used to run into the bedroom, shut the door, and cry with laughter. We used to hear a thump from the other room, a shriek of pain, and a 'God damn,' and my mother and aunt would jump into the bedroom like a shot."

January 23

Abrams has been everywhere, seen everything. He says life was marvelous years ago. The women hang on every word. He speaks of characters from his past, coming and going. Ma recalls that he used to be a ladies' man, and he replies that he also remembers the bedbug bites. He says to Ma, "Drezzle, yesterday you crossed my room and your feet didn't touch the floor. You left by the window out into the open air. How did you do it?"

Ma thinks him poetic as well as scatterbrained. As the women prepare to leave, Ma stands up and sings "Glory and Fame to the Men of Old."

There are tears in Abrams' eyes as he turns to me. "How is it, young man, that your mother, a veritable jewel among women, is spending her remaining years living here in the Home? Wasn't there a small place for her in your house? Under the sink? On the piano? In a dresser drawer?"

January 30
We meet a Mrs. Moss, who walks one step and stops, one step and stops, with an aluminum brace. She tells Ma that Isaac Abrams tried to take his life again. "Abrams," she says, "is from Warsaw, where people very often destroy themselves in the middle of life."

Abrams had put his head into a plastic bag and nearly succeeded in suffocating himself. Ma and I go up to the infirmary and find him with a tube in a nostril. He is being fed medicine through one intravenous and fluids through another. His swollen face is lighted by two gray eyes. His smile dissolves incessantly into expressions of bitterness. Ma sits there looking at him as the other women come in and gather around in silence.

February 3
During the week, Ma wrote a letter to Gabe Pressman, the streetwise reporter from Channel 5. I don't even want

to know what her brief was about. My hope is that Pressman doesn't show up at the Home, for Ma's sake. I warn her that she's flirting with removal from the second floor to the fifth floor.

February 12
After his last attempt at suicide, Abrams has never recovered his full size. His pallor is ghastly. He stands at his bedside, lost in his clothes. I look at Ma. She is trembling. She can't hold back her tears. I begin to bawl, too.

February 16
Today Abrams is out of bed, dressed in a 1924 sports outfit. He's lost so much weight that the clothes he has pulled from a satchel in his closet have him looking like a vaudeville attraction. He doesn't seem to recognize us as he goes around the room in jerks and jolts. He opens his mouth, and a garble of words pours out. His eyelids start to flutter. Ma and I are afraid to stir. We don't want to disturb him. Abrams has developed a tic and is making terrible faces at Ma.

Ma insists that I phone Seligman's office so that she can speak to him. His secretary says that he can give her a minute, and we go down to see him. He is dressed in a black suit and a black tie. Beckoning us into his office without a hello, he opens another door, which leads into a small, oblong room without windows or furniture.

Ma, somewhat nervous, blurts out, "Mr. Seligman, there are sections of the Home, especially on the fifth floor, that are completely cut off from fresh air, and it makes one's head swim."

"Mrs. Mehler," he answers, "things don't happen suddenly. They pile up gradually, and as we can't mention it, we say nothing at all." Baring his teeth, he whispers, "Mrs. Mehler, are you being properly looked after on the fifth floor?"

Ma is alarmed and corrects him, saying that she isn't a patient on the fifth floor, that her room number is 223, on the second floor, that I am her son Leon, and that she has two other children, Ronald and Marion.

We leave Seligman's office. There were only a few women typing at desks before, but now there are a number of social workers, men and women, sitting on a row of seats fixed to the wall. Catching sight of us, they rise, making it difficult to pass through them. Seligman snaps his fingers, saying, "Off with you. Keep the passageway clear."

February 19
Ma and I look in on a therapy dance group led by Molly Schwartz, a senility social worker. "Up, down, and around," she calls, slapping her hands together with a small, round bell in each. Eight women and two men shuffle about, repeating, "Up, down, and around." They, too, hold small, round bells, and the tinkles are lively. "Dance it, dance it!" Molly Schwartz calls, showing them a turn. "Dance it, dance it," they call. "Now you're all dancing the charconne," Molly Schwartz shouts. "Now front and now back, now sideways to the left . . . smiling . . . smiling . . . heads up . . . good."

February 24
At three o'clock, Ma and I go down to the basement to a birthday party. Seligman is presenting a gold watch to

Bernard Lester, who is a hundred years old today. "Bernard, you have been with us since this building opened, twenty-five years ago. We grew along with you, and now we celebrate your first one hundred years just as our new annex nears completion."

The tables are set up with cake and wine. Mrs. Katz plays a mazurka on her violin as some of the elderly move about in time to the music.

Bernard Lester sits in a black silk bathrobe, his feet thrust into out-of-shape slippers. Thin as a scarecrow, with large baby-blue eyes, he pooh-poohs the gold watch. "The whole schmear stinks," he says. "The same jokes, the same songs, and the same faces."

Ma shouts into his ear. "How old are you, Mr. Lester?"

"Over twenty-one," he retorts, and everyone laughs.

"How do you like your new gold watch, Mr. Lester?"

"Better than last year's fountain pen."

Rabbi Bernstein comes in and speaks a few words. "Everything is clear. To live to be one hundred is a great gift. What is the justice of that? God created life, and you, Bernard Lester, have no right to complain, as you are so special."

Ma has been expecting Isaac Abrams at the party, but he hasn't come down. Rumors begin circulating. A social worker calls me aside and whispers that they had nailed Abrams' window shut but that he went next door and jumped out of Mr. Rubin's window.

March 4

A stiff is wheeled into the elevator, the feet sticking out of the bottom of a sheet. A portion of the head remains uncovered, and Ma recognizes Mrs. Davenport, from the second floor, and speaks to her. "Lilly," she says, "I heard you're not feeling so good. We didn't see you at dinner this week." Ma introduces me. "Lilly, this is my son Leon." She tells the dead Mrs. Davenport not to worry—that she'll soon be up and around again.

In the hallway, Mr. Schultz, a smallish man with a limp, reminds Ma that it's four o'clock and that in an hour it will be five o'clock—dinnertime.

Aunt Lena

◇

AFTER PA DIED my aunt Lena and uncle
Albert took us in to live with them over the
summer. My aunt Lena menaced Cousin
Sonny with her lower teeth. Would she bite
him? Neckless, his hair combed with Mazola oil, he
snarled back. A Rudolph Valentino. Bessarabian eyes like
Stalin. Handsome maybe. The apple of her eye.

"Go out and break a leg!" she screamed. "He's very
good in arithmetic," she confided to Ma. "Having money
isn't enough. You've got to know how to add, no?"

Cousin Lillian sat in a corner, unable and aimless,
erupting periodically into a gnashing fury of self-
criticism. "Why don't I have dates?" she declared, as if we
all were guilty of something. Immediately after she settled into a benign melancholy, humming "If I had a

talking picture . . .", then passed into a bit of sunshine, a sudden spate of sardonic smiles.

"She's always eating Lovenests," said my aunt, thinking out loud. "Maybe she'll get married next year. Didn't Mrs. Fatman's daughter marry an engineer last month? . . . If a person borrows money they should pay back, no? Money unreturned is the way it is."

Cousin Mildred skipped in, older than Cousin Lillian and younger than Cousin Sonny. Black-haired, clutching a Hershey bar and licking it around so no one else would want any of it. "Take a glass of malted," cooed my aunt. Since my father died Ma was strangely haunted. My aunt looked at Cousin Sonny, the oldest. Instead of homework he was thinking he was invisible down in Mrs. Fatman's bloomers, again.

"Why when he has to go does he need advice from a psycho? Which hand should he use? And at a hundred dollars an hour no less! When we came to this country what did we do? We knew going to the toilet was to go. Simple." She called him "golem" and it sounded like "gay-lum." I couldn't see Cousin Sonny as a happy-lum somehow. My aunt went on: "If he fails his tests what will he be? Who? What is it? Can he get on Civil Service? He's weak in calculus, at least . . ." Frowning at Ma she growled, "Drezzle, what are you mixing around in the strawberries for? Take the top ones. What will be left for Albert and the children?"

Cousin Sonny sat moping at the table, wobbling his head yes and no in front of some chicken on a plate. He absolutely hated chicken and was preparing to make an independent decision by not eating any. My aunt said, "Eat." Mooning at the ceiling he wiggled his behind in a sort of Morse code, "no." Hitting the table a blow, she bawled, "Eat, or I'll knock your head off." Sonny, without a head! He took a small piece and slowly chewed and everything got nice and smooth again. Then he spat it out on the table, smirking triumphantly. My aunt threw herself at him for all her hard years. She held his nose with one hand and when he opened his mouth for air, she put pieces of chicken in with the other, commanding, "Eat or I'll knock your block off!" Sonny had waited too long to make an independent decision. Really, he was being helped through his meal and actually it was for the best anyway. Lamb chops had to be chewed up and down, didn't they . . . and swallowed, and what was wrong with swallowing up and down in the long run? It helped you, the vitamins, didn't it?

Dropping Sonny's nose, my aunt fixed Ma with a bland stare. "Drezzle, did you know the Smiths were robbed last night? Someone broke into the skylight and took a fur coat and money. . . . They say the police know who did it and who helped from the inside. . . ." The clock gave a loud tick at ten and she said, "Sonny, take a bath. . . . Papa is coming up from the store soon." Sonny got up because sooner or later he had to. He liked to sink into the tub and say something underwater.

Uncle Albert came up thinking to himself. A plain man, his eyes, the color of his hair and skin, seemed to have lost something. He brooded at Ma. Searching into a forest. Then he stood and looked at the wall for a while. He sat down and ate with both hands, reading the newspaper, bristling at something in the Business Opportunity section. He finished eating and stared at the wall again, dancing the little wallpaper flowers into cockroaches. Then he sang a muffled tune: "Toy doy doy doy doy doy doy," goose-pimpling me no end.

My aunt was a butterfly now, fluttering around my uncle, snitching about the strawberries on the bottom and

Sonny, weak in calculus, and what would become of him? Uncle continued "toy doying . . ." each "doy" dropping like a damp coin.

Sonny finished talking underwater, got out of the tub, and Lillian got in with Mildred and a Hershey bar. Then they got out and my aunt said, "Let Leon get in now before the water runs out." I screamed I didn't want to get into that mudpack and "I won't!" Ending her butterflying she said acidly to Ma, "Leon is spoiling Sonny's summer. Edison is rich enough," she added as she shut the lights hard and ordered everyone off to bed.

I could hear my aunt bumping around in the dark. She was a butterfly again . . . their bedsprings creaking endlessly while my uncle tried to remember something . . . "Toy doy doy doy doy doy . . ."

Penny Plain

◇

IN PARIS, Ma had an old picture postcard of Maurice stretched out on a sofa in the style of 1913. Long and handsome, lying in Edwardian splendor (their friends called him "the Doll"), with his chocolate eyes and vanilla teeth, ready to leap off the sofa into the Bourse and make a million. He leaped into the mating season with a handlebar mustache and black curly hair waving from the postcard as if to say "Marry me, Drezzle." But instead Maurice ran away with the charismatic Rosie to the United States. Rosie sent Ma a "Good-bye, Drezzle, we're going to America" postcard with a picture of herself and Maurice aboard the steamship *Berengaria.*

I've often thought that if Maurice Miller had married Ma, Ronald, Marion, and I would each have been someone else. Who knows what?

Ma met my father, Max, in Paris, married him, and came to the United States on the *Leviathan,* the largest ship in the world at the time. My brother Ronald and I were born in Paris and my sister Marion was born in New York, in the Bronx. My father was a good man and resembled the cowboy actor Tom Mix. Tall and stern. When at thirty-six my father drowned in the freak accident, Ma became haunted. She believed, of all things, that a certain Polansky was continually following her from an appetizing store. And if there was one there must be others. She said to me, "There could only be one explanation. Swimming along with this big fish Polansky must be a shoal of little fish . . . detectives!" "A fine kettle of fish," I laughed.

Ma complained the same way to my sister Marion. "No one believes me. They follow me everywhere." Ma wanted me to have them investigated and arrested. I asked, "How long has Polansky been after you?" "Months," she said. "I looked up Polansky in the phone book and there were two hundred and forty-five Polanskys in the listing, and why from an appetizing store?" Ma was very sensitive.

Ma's ladies' auxiliary was having a bingo bash at our house with some friends, and they spoke about the late Maurice Miller, now called Morris Miller, and his wife, the charismatic Rosie Miller.

Mrs. Kelly gathered the bingo numbers and began a new round. "N–12." She remembered how it was and how Rosie Miller behaved toward her late husband Morris. Rosie's eyes had a haunting way of looking in instead of looking out, always putting Morris down as a failure. "I don't think she'll ever be much better than she is." Mrs. Kelly didn't care for Rosie Miller at all with her fast little legs and her crepe de chine blouse.

Mr. Green had bingo and collected his pennies, saying, "As Morris would say, 'Laugh it up.'"

"Morris was a workingman," Ma said. "He wasn't 'the Doll' anymore in this country. It was after the war and other men were diving into business, while Morris still worked at ladies' garments. If he lost at cards his wife Rosie called him 'Wanamaker,' after the successful department store on Fourteenth Street. She would give him a penny a game to play. Morris had said that the time would come when the garment industry would pay time and a half after a regular day's work, double time on Saturdays, and triple time on Sundays, Christmas, and Yom Kippur. G–13."

"O–26," Mrs. Kelly called. "They both used to be like two turtledoves, always billing and cooing."

Mr. Green remembered that after a while it cooled off and they took things more slowly, the mystery of Rosie no longer new for Morris. He then spoke about Morris's death. . . . "He never came out of his daze . . . he was like a sleepwalker. . . ." Mr. Green hit bingo again and I could hear him whisper to Ma with a tender almost loving smile. "Drezzle, our life will work itself out," and to reassure her he drew a tableau of a carefree future of smiling promises. "N–49."

"Overtime is good enough," Mr. Cohn said. "Rosie Miller ate Morris up alive. B–2."

"On the other hand," Mrs. Siegel said, "Rosie could be sweetness itself. G–38."

"I'm a man like this," Mr. Cohn said: "I like people but not too much. G–31."

Mr. Green had a sense of humor. "Drezzle, I'm making you the beneficiary of my life insurance. It's little enough to give you. I'll abandon everything for you. N–14."

Ma was in high spirits, having been winning pennies

like mad. She spoke cheerfully about Morris in the old days. "In Paris, Morris was happy-go-lucky and devil-may-care and blessed with a healthy appetite for the pleasures of this world and a total absence of interest in the next. He was the gayest and the least reverent of our friends, and no one was so safe as to be free from his laughter."

Mrs. Klar, who hadn't said much, spoke. "Yes, Morris was a handsome man indeed. The more Rosie worried him, the better-looking he got, especially his hair. It waved and struggled, curling around his head like sheep's wool. It 'waved' at passersby, as if to say, 'I'm Morris. I'm not finished yet!' B-16."

Ma's mood changed and her voice was insecure again. She said that yesterday a well-dressed man wearing a derby approached Honeywell Avenue. I said, "So what, Ma?" "He was too well-dressed for the neighborhood," she worried. "I'm sure it was Polansky." Then Ma leaned over and whispered so as not to divert the bingo company, "You don't believe me, do you?" I called out, "I-14!"

I remembered a time back when Rosie Miller opened a neighborhood candy store on East 180 Street with her husband Morris and their two sons, Wally and Seymour, plus Ida Lentle from Flatbush, a twin sister to Rosie, almost a duplicate, lean at ninety pounds, with the same quick energy. Ida Lentle didn't get along with Morris at all. I turned to Ma and reminded her about some of the "penny plain" days. "The two cents plain days . . ." Ma laughed. "Remember the time that the five of them worked in the one candy store, the time that Morris chased the kids out when they hung around too long for a nickel's worth of Indian nuts and as a result the parents stopped coming in for newspapers and cigarettes? Then there was Ida Lentle's sarcasm about Morris leaning against the counter and sticking his finger into the syrup of the malted milk while serving a customer. Remember when Ida called him 'a born slob' in front of all the customers? He always managed to drop half the mustard and sauerkraut on the floor before he'd get it on the hot dog."

Mrs. Klar liked Morris and spoke of him as a good man: "He was so humble, and just because it dwelt within him, he never regarded it as a virtue. O–64."

Mrs. Kelly had another point of view. "Dear Morris was something you'd pick off a Christmas tree with his great white hair and ready smile. G–58."

Mrs. Wilkins had bingo and pulled in her pennies from the middle of the table. "I–20." She recalled Morris's folly. "He got carried away. His plan was to make enough income to open another candy store nearby in case things slowed down in the first. The two boys, Wally and Seymour, could work there afternoons and evenings, while Morris would open in the morning and keep busy at the toy counter. Rosie would take care of the first store until the afternoon when the boys would take over and he would join Rosie. Ida Lentle would commute between the two stores, depending upon where the most customers hung out."

"Up the creek," I said. "B–3."

One day Morris decided to surprise Rosie and Ida Lentle by adding another counter. They accused him of starting to move into grocery goods with Saint John's bread, ladyfingers, charlotte russe cakes, plus a table for hot coffee. "Soon he'll make a nightclub in the store," Rosie wailed. "Why must he always help himself to a cigar from the stock?" Ida Lentle quipped. She was constantly watching Morris so she could tattle on him to Rosie, who once saved her from a kick in the behind by Morris.

Ma called "O–55" with a fresh card. "Listen," she said, "Wally and Seymour began eating up all the jelly beans and the Tar Babies without bothering to reorder. Then they ate the Baby Ruths. They would sleep late and lose the morning newspaper sales, and as a result they leaked into the time schedule of the other three."

"Sometimes," Mrs. Wilkins continued, "all five of them overlapped with more of them than customers. The bell on the door would tinkle, and if someone came in it was like the bell at ringside, all five jumping around for one egg cream. G–60."

This day Ma came in to talk with Morris a bit. The small talk soon widened and Ma's and Morris's hearts drew closer as they reawakened bygone memories.

". . . and do you remember how we called you 'the Doll'?" Morris was carried away, and sighing he made the mistake of saying, "Love's labour's lost, Drezzle. . . ." Rosie heard and stopped the electric malted machine, directing her talk to her sister Ida. "Mademoiselle Drezzle's bumping around into Morris again," a signal for Ida Lentle to grab a broom and start sweeping left and right like a crazy *yezababa* gone mad, and that was the last time Ma went into the candy store.

Ma had a routine going to bed after Pa died. She would go into her bedroom, lock it, and put two or three chairs against the door. Under her bed she had a pepper shaker, and she seriously believed that one night Polansky would break into her room and that she would blind him with pepper and shout for help. Ma had a lot of imagination.

Mr. Cohn said, "Morris expected that after the store got on its feet he'd put in a lunch counter. Then it all folded up like a dream. Morris's 'season' started at ladies' garments and they closed the store altogether and that was the end of two cents plain. . . . N–33."

I called "I–23" followed by a reminiscence. "A strange atmosphere brooded over that candy store on East One hundred eightieth Street. Laughter never seemed to shine in that room full of Tootsie Rolls, Milky Ways, and those fine, silver-papered Hershey's Kisses. . . ." Ma said she never found any laughter to equal those of the exciting bingo games and the enfolding warmth of her friends. She was forty-two and of a spirit quite ageless, especially when winning pennies.

"A short life and a merry one," Mrs. Kelly laughed, toasting Ma with a spot of Ma's port. Mrs. Kelly was herself a widow, whose husband Jim, a fireman, had died a few years earlier at a four-alarm fire on Boston Road.

As Morris got older he looked fantastic, with his full snow-white hair, apple-red cheeks, and his blue, blue eyes and penetrating gaze. His height and bodily strength gave him the appearance of an actor from the theater instead of a partnership in a candy store. When he died, I thought of him as an American flag with the red, white, and blue of him, whereas his wife Rosie, alive and kicking, dried up like a fig.

Personally, I liked Uncle Morris and regretted the time I hurt him. It had all been a mistake. My brother Ronald had bought a suit at Howard Stores and was given a fedora hat free with his purchase even though he never wore a hat. Uncle Morris was visiting, and during the evening I took the hatband out of Ronald's hat, trying to get it to fit my head. Only I grabbed the wrong hat. When Uncle Morris got ready to leave our house, his hat was sizes too large and it fell down over his eyes to his nose. Poor Uncle Morris. Everybody was in stitches. Ma said, "Morris, your head shrunk." I reminded Ma of the hat incident during the bingo game, and she burst into tears remembering Morris and how he'd become the village idiot at every turn.

Everybody expected that Mr. Green, a widower, would marry Ma sooner or later. His constant sophistry was a pain.

"If a husband were to live a hundred years," Mr. Green said, "he would never know anything about the real existence of his wife. What I need from my wife is the truth. N–48."

We never knew whether Mr. Green was joking or not. "I have become enamored of Drezzle," he said, "for a lack of luck at love and my lonely life." The smile on his lips dissolved into expressions of bitterness taken from many deceptions and disillusionments or swinging moods from winning or losing at bingo.

Mrs. Kelly said, "Anyway, I'm certain that Drezzle had taken a fancy to Morris. She had a picture over the mantelpiece of Rosie and Morris crossing on the *Berengaria,* and now he's gone . . . whisht. God bless us! O–70."

"Rosie's a bantamweight, a gamecock," Mr. Cohn said. "The minute she has something to holler about she begins to shine. She can lay down in the rain and never catch cold. N–70."

Mr. Green explained the way things are: "Two plain people may marry and nobody bothers them. Sometimes one of the two shines and the other stays plain. Some beauties stand frozen in one spot, while a cockeyed one moves around like crazy. There are those who come to the wedding bed homely and are in endless atonement under the covers. This is sex appeal. B–10.”

Mrs. Kelly gave a yawn. “If you say so, Mr. Green. A month in the country would make us all young.”

Mr. Green was kidding Ma. “Drezzle, the fact remains that Rosie is probably one of the most brilliantly beautiful women ever seen in the Bronx. N–47.”

Mr. Cohn couldn’t stand it anymore. “I’ve seen many women and Rosie Miller looks like a gibbon. G–55.”

Ma came to life suddenly, offering everybody some biscuits and port.

There was a knock on the door and Rosie Miller herself entered, dressed in a cape with a pointed bonnet, a gnomelike hat trimmed with plush and artificial flowers. She was accompanied by a retinue of large housewives from the Ladies’ Auxiliary Society. Ma was like a gazelle, doelike and frightened to the quick with the stampeding women who had just arrived for bingo. I ran for chairs to seat them in. Ma not only was walleyed but also a head taller than Rosie Miller. Imbalance was the word for Ma. “Rosie,” Ma said, “you’re all wet. The rain’s been coming down in sheets, so here, dry yourself at the steam pipe and join us for bingo. I’ll get Leon to make some tea and bring you back to life.”

Rosie Miller, sitting next to the large tightly packed housewives, said, “My beautiful ones . . .” She winked roguishly and smiled at Ma, calling her Mademoiselle Drezzle, then turned toward Mr. Green, saying, “. . . I had just given up my place on the Avenue de Chatillon and had moved to another hotel on the Rue du Faubourg-Montmartre. Poor Maurice! He could hardly eke out a living." Rosie Miller paused for a moment. "He was a great lover," she added with a sigh. "Once in a dreary little hotel room he made love to me seven times the same evening. N–34."

Mr. Klar said, "Seven times? Unbelievable. Morris must have had the capacity of a Greek god. B–40."

Mr. Wilkins added, "I had no idea Morris's love was so deep. O–12."

Mr. Cohn had the last word. ". . . and so to bed, one would hope, with the man who made it all possible. G–61."

Rosie Miller glared at Ma. "Don't worry about us, Drezzle. Only last Saturday night Mrs. Winston lost her pocketbook in your house. What have you to say about that?"

"N–44." Ma had bingo again and picked up her pennies. Rosie stamped her feet, declaring that there was twenty dollars and change missing from Mrs. Winston's purse, and the large housewives echoed the tumult, repeating, ". . . Missing from Mrs. Winston's purse!" A pecking order.

"G–39," Rosie Miller growled. "Mademoiselle Drezzle, I noticed that someone removed your Orphans' Box from the wall last week. Yes, the tin tongue was bent over to let the coins tumble out."

Ma ignored Rosie's remarks and went on to talk about Morris in Paris:

"We went to the theater regularly in those days and there were so many museums to visit and of course we ate frequently in restaurants and cafés and went dancing a lot too. We were going to settle down together. O–62."

"Settle down?" Mr. Cohn said. "I would never settle down again. I'm a widower and meet some very exciting new people all the time. I–4."

Rosie Miller snarled, "A watch is missing! O–70."

Mrs. Kelly laughed. "She's a terrible bully. I–12."

Mrs. Klar said, "Settle down, Mr. Cohn? You are a charming man, but I must say you're always here playing bingo. Where do you meet all your new people? B–3."

"Weep on, Drezzle," Mrs. Kelly said. "Rosie Miller's a raging devil, and if you only looked crooked at her, you're sure of a punch in the nose. I–17."

Ma decided it was time to end the bingo game, and as chairwoman made the announcement, "I declare closed." Rosie Miller moved in quickly. "Drezzle, what do you declare closed, the closet?" It took Ma a half hour to recover her composure and parliamentary procedure. "I declare the Ladies' Auxiliary Society closed."

Getting ready to leave, Mrs. Kelly said, "Oh, isn't this a nice end to a quiet glass of wine and a biscuit. . . . Good night, Drezzle dear, we've had a right good time together with all that bingo. By the by, who's this Polansky bloke?"

It was Mr. Green's last visit to our house with his two daughters, Tessy and Milly, and his password was still, "Drezzle, give the girls some bananas and cream." When it was Ma's turn to visit them, it was impossible to find even a piece of candy. I knew apple pie must be hiding somewhere in that house. Lurking about I managed to find Mr. Green's cache up on top of their china closet. I quickly piled one chair on top of another and grabbed a handful of pie for myself and threw some to my brother Ronald waiting down below. I had to eat fast before the two daughters ran in and caught me eating their apple pie near the ceiling.

Mr. Green had been planning to live with Ma in our house now that they were both single again, but he never spoke about marriage. He grabbed Tessy and Milly and ran over to our house. "Drezzle, we'll split the rent and food in half, you'll cook, and it will be good for all the children." Ma would have had to work for Marion, Ronald, myself, and the two sisters, plus Mr. Green to boot. A sneaky free-love proposal, but even so Ma didn't get a chance to say no to him because the demure Rosie Miller came into the house wearing an old gray Persian lamb, all drenched in perfume and powdered up in the pale style of a mime. Moving her purple-painted lips she said, "My dear Mr. Green, you do resemble my late husband Morris, may he rest in peace. It never occurred to me that he would pass away. A sudden hemorrhage, a flow of blood . . . and gone. . . . A lovely man, our union, though rocked by many storms, endured."

An amazing thing that Rosie Miller, with all her wrinkles and crinkles, could charm and capture Mr. Green and that they were now living at her house with his two daughters, Tessy and Milly, and her two sons, Wally and Seymour. A coo-coo nest. Rosie Miller was one of those people who moved around so quickly you never could see what she really looked like.

Ma was down in the dumps, but not because she had passed up Mr. Green's early proposal, but more so because Rosie Miller had moved so quickly and brought Ma painful memories of that old postcard with Morris and her sailing away on the steamship *Berengaria*. I tried to cheer up Ma, saying, "Listen, I found a satchel in the train the other day and when I brought it home and opened it, guess who was inside? Mr. Green and Rosie Miller!"

My sister Marion understood Ma better than Ronald or I. Marion said that Ma would have been wasted on the likes of Mr. Green and his two daughters, that there were hundreds of Mr. Greens all over the place, and that Ma was special, having lived such an innocent and loving life.

I tell Ma that Rosie Miller is a hobgoblin which is even worse than a regular goblin.

Mr. Green had stopped coming around for Ma's bingo games, and a month later Mrs. Kelly announced that Mr. Green had "kicked the bucket!" He started to die soon after he and Rosie married. Hungry to the end, he got dressed up and went down to the Isaac Gellis Delicatessen on the corner. He passed away the color of pale corned beef and Rosie gave up the large housewives and everything went back to normal between good and evil.

The Dream

◊

TUESDAY NIGHT AT NINE, the gorgeous, black-haired Mrs. Farinello from apartment 2-G stood up, pulling her bottom out of the stuffing of an easy chair in our living room. She said, "Excuse me," to Ma and went swaying down the buff-colored hallway to the toilet on the left. I ran out of my room in sneakers . . . silently, straight to the toilet door, bent down on one knee, turned my head sideways, closed my right eye, looked in through the keyhole with my left eye, and saw Mrs. Farinello holding her dress up high flying to heaven on the toilet bowl. The same Mrs. Farinello who said, "Yes, thank you," and "No, thank you," and "How do you do, my dear?" sitting with her legs apart in ecstasy, smiling and peeing out of a crazy crack with black whiskers . . . but she hadn't turned the lock! She didn't lock the door! She had left it open! She didn't shut it! Open! I fell in halfway and she couldn't believe it seeing me flat on the floor. She hopped off the bowl. She tried to kick the door shut with her foot. I ran out backward. On all fours. All the way. Backward into my room, under the bed . . . would she tell my mother? Maybe I was playing ball and happened to fall in. And if she took me to jail, I would tell the jury that it was a pinkish, reddish, brownish, blackish, and peeing as though its heart were breaking. . . .

I came out from under the bed, shut the light, and looked out the window to see if the sexless Hoffman sisters across the way were getting undressed yet. The Hoffman family was shaking back and forth getting ready to go to bed. Undressing time, they swayed back and forth each in his own window, the father shaking in his window on the right, his eyes shut, his lips moving silently. Millie, Christopher's younger sister, swayed in the second window from the right. Christopher's mother, middle-aged, tied together by a network of veins and arteries, rocked back and forth in window number three. Christopher, himself, the son in his late teens and the oldest of the children, practiced saxophone in number four. He swayed "Barcarole" and "The Flying Dutchman." He closed with "Humoresque," shook the sax as though he were dancing with it, put it away in a black box, then took it out several times again, doing an encore of sorts, soloing with make-believe name orchestras.

Mollie, the older, fatter sister, fourteen years old, quivered like Jell-O, her hips bobbling about in sloppy gypsy to Christopher's music. In a half hour they would all shake and shuffle right into bed. Lights out.

Underneath Christopher's window lived Rosie and Tillie Cohen, who were out tooling it up with Harry and

Lew, their "no hands" motorcycle boyfriends. It took minutes to get anywhere by motorcycle and only one minute to get to Bronx Park.

Bronx Park was full of unemployed "droolies," hobgoblins that jumped out of the shadows and opened their flies, rolled their eyes, put their thumbs in their ears, wiggled their fingers, and moaned, "Ooooooeeeeeeee." Only last week a droolie had actually hidden behind Rosie Cohen and her boyfriend Harry. Harry and Rosie were lying in the grass making love when Rosie discovered a third hand on her thigh. A third hand, clammy, with fingers racing like a centipede playing piano right up to her spot and out again, charging around her backside, then up and down her leg. Some hand, thought Rosie. It can't be Harry's. "Harry!" she screamed, suddenly aware that it wasn't his. The droolie jumped out of the bushes, put his thumbs in his ears, wiggled his fingers, and shrieked, "Ooooooooeeeeeee" at the top of his lungs. Harry staggered around, struggling to put his hard-on away and zipper up.

The motorcycle boys must have learned their lesson, and they began taking the Cohen girls up the Bronx River Parkway instead, where the standard of living was higher. Anyway when I looked in the window the house was still dark.

Living next door to us was the Murphys' bedroom, where I could hear Mrs. Murphy singing "Galway Bay." Taking a chair I stood on it and listened, my ear flat against the wall. Three feet from the ceiling I looked through a needle hole I had carefully drilled a week before. A pink breast with a nipple! Mrs. Murphy's! Hanging there in the peephole! Singing "Galway Bay" three feet from the ceiling, six feet from the floor. Oh, the good, fat Mrs. Murphy's undressed at last! One breast?

Wait! Maybe she'll move back a little . . . she wouldn't high-jump into the air? I got down from the chair, bent over, and looked into a second hole two feet and four inches from the floor . . . another breast! Halfway between the first two holes I opened my third and last hole and looked through . . . a third breast . . . three breasts roughly six and three-quarter feet apart? Just breasts? I closed the holes with fresh gum and moved the chair over to the steam pipe, taking a box from under the bed, putting it on the chair, holding onto the steam pipe, and pulling a white flat cork out of the ceiling. I looked up to see if Mrs. Schindler was crawling about. . . . I corked up the ceiling and returned to the pinholes, removed the chewing gum, and looked through again . . . just breasts singing "Galway Bay." Maybe they were really wax breasts set there to catch someone by her policeman husband, hoping to make an arrest and get a promotion to detective. He always said, "It's no use your fighting with the Marquis of Queensberry rules. I'd grab your balls and squeeze. I don't care if you wrestle, do judo or karate all the time, remember I've got your balls in my fist." Like that time in the Bronx woods when he made out he was sleeping in the grass next to Mrs. Murphy, who sat with her dress up, smiling, while multitudes of park bums rose up from the bushes in the dark and crawled toward her on their knees and elbows, clutching massive hard-ons.

Adjusting her thighs so they could see under better, Mrs. Murphy hummed "Come Back to Killarney," as the first few unemployed came up and crept under her dress, half shoved by those in the rear. Grumbling and bickering broke out immediately in a push and pull for place and position, when suddenly Bill Murphy, the cop, jumped up and began to beat those bumping about under her dress with the butt of his service revolver. Howling dreadfully, they tumbled out, holding their heads in great pain, shrieking, "I didn't do it. He did . . ." whoever "he did" was. This started a panic, with stampeding bums trying to protect their heads and genitals at the same time. Bill Murphy, the avenger, struck savagely, left and right with his gun, chopping off and flopping hard-ons all over the field. Scattered cock fell white in the moonlight, their owners wailing piteously, "What will we do now?" as they ran around trying to get away from the possessed policeman, feeling about in the grass at the same time slipping and searching for their lost members.

Some of the hard-ons took instant root in the ground, growing into thirty-foot erections with hundreds of new uncircumcised penises growing off the top like bananas. A number of bums climbed up and were fitting themselves for size, naturally taking bigger ones than they'd lost, throwing the smaller ones down to the desperate rabble below. Many of them came down with brand-new two-foot salamis, dragging them around in the melee, tripping over them as they ran. Others were using fallen cock for weapons, striking each other in the face and head, adding to the general misery and commotion. Finally Bill Murphy captured them all. Lining them up and placing them under arrest he said, "You bums know the penalty for this. I could have shot and killed all of you for what you were trying to do. You've no one else to blame but yourselves; those of you who are first offenders will be out before the week is over. I'll be down here looking for you. You may get another chance to see my wife's bottom but you'll pay a price for it." He then gave out Band-Aids and cough drops until he could get them to the station house and medical aid. Hands over their heads they marched out of the park with Bill Murphy at their rear.

Except me. I was still under Mrs. Murphy's dress. I

never came out. "Murphy's a strange man," she said; "whenever I think I know him, there's something different. Listen, you'd better hurry up and finish. If he finds you under there, he'll shoot your balls off with his forty-five." I ran out, leaving Mrs. Murphy in the bushes with new droolies rising up all around her in the dark. Oh, boy, wait till Murphy gets back. . . .

Across the yard the Hoffmans hadn't gone to bed. The father was chasing something, maybe a three-inch cockroach, from room to room as if he were skating after it. Mollie, the fat sister, was doing the Charleston, shaking about underneath a sheer nightgown, her sheep's eyes half shut in heat; "Charleston, Charleston, one two three . . ." The father finally stepped on the roach, crushing it with a loud dry crack . . . startling the rest of the family listening . . . trembling into Christopher's room, holding each other around. Christopher's father took a bottle of whiskey out of the bureau drawer, pulled out the cork with his teeth, and took a swallow, turning his head up to the ceiling, his Adam's apple moving up and down once. One eye turned red, the other yellow, then both filled with tears as he said, "Ah-h-h-h."

Christopher peeped into the bureau mirror at the two sisters starting to dance again in their transparent nightgowns, slapping their behinds, warming up into a "black bottom you've gottem . . ." Then they did a two-step, stopping and bumping, then stepping again. They moved about the room, bumping into Christopher every chance they could. Mollie kept saying something like, "You show us yours and we'll show you ours." Then both sisters hissed, "Show us yours and we'll show you ours." They didn't wait. They pushed him down to the floor, out of sight below the sill. Millie must have been on top. I could just barely see her cherubic bottom bobbing about like a butterfly. When she got off, Mollie got on. Someone yelled from upstairs. "That dirty slob Christopher's doing it to both his kid sisters!" Lights went on all over on both sides of the yard. Someone shouted, "Call the police!" Tenants crowded to their windows in varied stages of undress, asking who's doing it to both his kid sisters? Where? Mrs. Schindler, upstairs, exclaimed bitterly, "Now the bearded father's got the young girl and the mother and Mollie are doing something dreadful with Christopher's face. . . . I can't tell you what! They're all naked, on all fours, going around saying, 'Halvah.' I can guarantee you the mother will never show her face in the street around here again." Someone threw a match into their apartment and in seconds the windows were full of flames. Cries of, "Help us–s–s–ssssss," sputtered and curled up like a strip of bacon.

The Hoffmans had burned up in the middle of their orgy, leaving the 180 Street crowd hypnotized, staring, hoping, that something would continue to screw in the ashes. They never even saw Millie fly across the yard with her butterfly ass right into my window, the only one saved from the fire. I closed the window and pulled the shade down tight. "Christopher's gone," was all she said, still in her nightgown. I got her a chicken leg and some cream soda. Then I gave her a pair of dungarees and one of my shirts, large on her but stylish, with the shirttails outside the pants. Then we went out to the street and took the crosstown bus to Loew's Paradise Theatre on the Grand Concourse. We got two seats in the orchestra just in time for Oscar at the organ rising out of a golden choir screen with a bacchanal relief of fat Bronx nymphs being shot with bow and arrow by flying cherubs flanked by satyrs in merry-go-round pursuit. Unscrewing from the center of the choir screen, a high column turned, encrusted with crystal, splashing reds, blues, and magentas as another shaft rose out of the first, turning the opposite way, showering yellow and orange all over the theater.

The gold-and-silver organ turned out of the top of the last column . . . around . . . and . . . around . . . purring and humming, imitation bells ringing, crickets rubbing, canaries chirping, as Oscar's purple jacket came up with the organ seat, his long arms sweeping over the shelves of keys, buttons, and knobs. Then Oscar's head slid out of the top of the jacket full of yellow curls, smiling with a mouthful of Chiclets, whispering vaudevillesqué: "I love you all! I love you all!" Throwing kisses to the crowd, he stood thirty feet above the orchestra, and bowing low he said, "Good evening, ladies and gentlemen. Allow me to welcome you on behalf of the management of the Loew's Paradise Theatre here in the West Bronx. I am Oscar," . . . then unzipping his fly, he howled . . . "and this is my organ!" Then he put his thumbs in his ears, wiggled his fingers, and moaned "OOOOOOOOOOooooooEEEEE eeeeee" over the loudspeaker.

Lenin in Bronx Park

◇

ABOUT THE GIRL. I knew only that her name was Molly and that she sang with all her heart and that listening, I was lost. It was a mixed-up time. I met her in Miller's Ice Cream Parlor. We walked around in the Bronx Woods and there was a full moon out and a scent of clover. I didn't get back home until four A.M. Months later I met her again and she wanted to know whatever had happened to me. I told her I'd been knocking on her door, number 4-B, ever since I'd met her and no one was ever home. "That's 'cause I live in 3-B," she said. "Apartment 4-B has been empty all year."

Molly was exciting to see, blond hair, shoulder-length with bangs, lavender eyes, and jet-black eyelashes, and an artist's model to boot at the Art Students League. She was an orphan and had been raised in an orphanage some-where in Boston. We met a third time at a "cultural dance," and afterward we spent the rest of the evening on top of the tenement where I lived. Nobody had enough money to go to a hotel in those days. Sex on a rooftop was how it was in the Bronx.

"It was never as good with anybody else, ever."

"I don't believe you. It isn't true. Swear to me."

"I swear. Never with anybody, you darling, you sweet . . ."

We were in love and I brought her home to meet my mother and my sister Marion, who were asleep in the high-riser they shared. I woke them up by turning on the lights. Since Pa died Ma had an open-door policy; anyone who rang the bell was welcome to our house. "Sit a little. Stay awhile. Have something to eat. Come freely and leave something of the happiness you bring." So it came as no surprise to me to hear Ma invite Molly to sleep over. Besides Marion was glad to see that I didn't bring home a "dog." They welcomed Molly, who promptly jumped into bed with Marion and Ma.

The next day Molly moved in with us permanently. Ma moved my brother Ronald into the foyer, and Molly and I shared the bedroom. We lived on the fifth floor and our window overlooked the Bronx Park Zoo. At seventeen Molly was already a political person and many times she'd return home with Little Lenin Library pamphlets. During supper she told my brother that in another year or two there wouldn't be a single woman collective farmer in the Soviet Union who wouldn't have her own cow.

Ma asked, "Where will they keep the cow? On the fire escape?" Ma didn't like me living with Molly. "A shame for the neighbors." She made some tea and took a word: "Someone should have warned Leon's grandfather,

David, about fleeting passions and free love." My grandmother had had thirteen children and Ma was number
nine.

It was actually my dentist, Ben S., who converted me
into the Party. It was hard to argue with his drill in my
mouth. He'd whisper, "Shhh, shh," to keep my voice
down low so that no one in the waiting room would think
we were overthrowing the government. "Listen," he
drilled, "we are fighting better than our fathers did and
our children will fight still better and they will win." He
was talking about socialism. It wasn't just the dentist;
quite a number of City College students were in the
political Left, and one of my livelier friends, whose as-
sumed name was "Walt Whitman," would chase out on
the street after a passing Cadillac with clenched fists
shouting, "Long live Stalin and the Scottsboro boys!"
Herbert Hoover was President then and there were long
breadlines.

Molly's friend, "Emma Lazarus," was going with a
Marxist and we had invited them for supper. We were in
the kitchen having soup when he suddenly exploded into
my ears, screaming, "Yes, I am a Trotskyite!" The soup
spurted out of my mouth. All of us in the Party had been
instructed not to socialize or have anything to do with
Trotskyites. And here was one sitting in my house eating
my food! "Come with me to the public library," he
brayed, "and I'll show you evidence of life under Stalin!"
"Emma Lazarus" had recently changed her name back to
Sophie Smith and was no longer a Marxist. She had
become a Freudian and sat smiling as if everything that
went on before was nothing. She said that Freud wrote
that fetishism was a penis substitute, adding that "happy
people don't make history."

Ma was a devil and since she made the meal, she asked

the Trotskyite why Trotsky as well as Lenin had ordered workers shot at Kronstadt when they wouldn't turn over produce to the Central Committee in Moscow and would Trotsky have been any different in power than Stalin? The supper was a shambles.

I visited my dentist, Ben S., who recommended that I read Stalin's fourth chapter on dialectics. He did my gums as he spoke: "Take frost as a thesis," he said. "If it gets hot, the ice melts and it becomes water . . . which is an antithesis to frost. Then if the water turns to steam, it becomes a new form again or a synthesis or the reverse, from steam to water to ice . . . thesis, antithesis, synthesis. . . ."

We had a large demonstration of several thousand people in Union Square. The police charged the mass meeting on horseback. Caught at the edge of the crowd I climbed a lamp pole to get out of the stampede. A crazy thing . . . I decided not to come down when ordered by a policeman. I was busy raising a hullabaloo up on top and I responded to the cheers of the throng spread out below me. The cops couldn't reach me and they called the fire department. I was the center of some kind of theater called trouble. I saw my life passing in front of me . . . "Abigail Adams," Molly, staying out nights, Ma and Marion and Ronald.

A police captain beckoned to me to come down while I still had a chance. He smiled up and assured me that he understood the pickle I was in. I was being hosed by a fire wagon and decided to slide down, as I was in danger of getting flushed off anyway by the force of the water. The rest happened so fast. I was thrown to the ground and beaten over the head by several cops at once and repeatedly kicked. The police told the *Daily News* that I had fallen off the pole. My picture made the front page.

Ben S. lectured me on ignorance. "What is the sky to you? A hole, Leon?" He clutched his head in both hands and swung it from left to right. He couldn't get over it. Such a revelation had suddenly become just too painful. He whispered into my ear as he drilled my tooth. "The bourgeois family will vanish as a matter of course when its complement vanishes and both will vanish with the vanishing of capital."

In our house "Tom Paine" was speaking about Picasso and the Impressionists. He said that Monet's paintings of the facade of the Rouen Cathedral reached a dead end, that this painting had become nothing more than a shallow surface of glittering color and that we now had a period vitiated by impotence, paralyzed by "art for art's sake." He attacked Manet, Seurat, and Matisse. Picasso was another matter. He had an unfailing attachment to the poor, the oppressed, the miserable, and the exploited.

Albert Laspira, alias Alexander Hamilton, a City College student, didn't agree with "Tom Paine," saying that Manet, Seurat, and Matisse painted works of art, and that it would take more than ideology to stifle their greatness. "As for Picasso," he said, "some critics have said that much of Picasso's nudes give the impression of graffiti on lavatory walls."

Ma came in to serve some hot chocolate. She asked "Tom Paine" why Stalin had rejected and returned the portrait Picasso had painted of him. "It was in all the newspapers that Stalin had called Picasso's art bourgeois and decadent." "Tom Paine" answered Ma that Picasso's various styles were in the comic mask of the bitter jester, indicating a sympathy with the poor and a secret hostility for the rich. "Alexander Hamilton" turned to my brother, who was "Patrick Henry" now, and in a ringing attack on the Soviet Union added that tired cliché that an apple by Cézanne was of more consequence artistically than the head of a Madonna by Raphael.

Molly bounced in again. She found me asleep on the sofa, in a bad mood. She kissed me to forestall the storm as though nothing was the matter. She hugged me against her breast, calling me her "good Bolshevik." She kept talking: "Darling. My all. Do you feel that I'm yours?" The endearments embarrassed me.

It was 1940 and Union Square was the place to be. We had a demonstration warning that Fascism was rapidly spreading without control throughout Europe, with signs reading JOIN THE LEAGUE AGAINST WAR AND FASCISM. Somebody threw a bottle at the mounted police, a horse on charge let off vapor and bursts of whinnying hysteria, the teeth showing, the foam on its bit, the tongue hanging out. A close-up of a horse on the sidewalk with a club-swinging cop in the saddle is a lot of action. The possibility of the beast smashing into me against a building or crashing a hoof and crushing the bones of my feet with the frenzied cop above ready to break my head. We ran into Woolworth's on Thirteenth Street, expecting the damned animal and "Ivan the Terrible" to follow and trample us. The horse knew what it was doing. We came out again . . . the frightened crowd was running in all directions away from the galloping horses. Crossing Union Square to get to the east side I was caught from behind by a cop who got me in a headlock and flipped me to the ground. While I was down and about to get up, another cop, at full run, took a flying kick into my right side. Many plainclothesmen shouted obscenities at the women. A gang of us locked arms and pushed ourselves against the police.

Ben S. spoke about Fascism while removing one of my front teeth, "Big business runs the world," he said, "but it already has one foot in the grave. Big business, with its trusts and monopolies and its ruthless exploitation of the people, is dying. . . ."

"Now he tells me," I mutter, spitting a mouthful of blood into the sink.

Molly hasn't been home for the past few days and I phoned her sister, "Betsy Ross," in Brooklyn. She had seen Molly at a meeting on Tuesday but didn't know where she was staying. Seconds later Molly comes in with "Emily Dickinson." They floated in like butterflies. They were both very pretty. Ma made them lunch. She asked where they had been. "Emily Dickinson" laughed and jokingly said, "Mrs. Mehler, that's called the sacred right of private property." Molly said, "We find in the *Nibelungenlied* that in her heart Kriemhild is as much in love with Siegfried as he is with her. Let us hope that the ranks of the leading women peasants will be swelled by the addition of fresh politically conscious peasant women."

I said, "Self-control and self-discipline are not slavery, not even in love."

My brother "Patrick Henry" agreed with me. "Dissoluteness in sexual life is bourgeois, is a phenomenon of decay."

"Listen to him," Molly laughed. "The oppressed sex is crushed economically because, no matter how democratic the state may be, the woman remains a 'domestic slave under capitalism, a slave of the bedroom, nursery, and kitchen.' "

Ma said, "Meyer Levine was an old Jew close to eighty who had been planning for a long time to go to Palestine to die. His wife didn't want to go with him because she felt she couldn't forsake the cemetery in Kovno where her entire family lay buried. On the other hand, without his wife, Meyer Levine would not migrate to the land of Israel. For how can a Jew leave for Palestine without his wife? You young people don't understand this."

Tonight, "Tom Paine" holds forth on "surplus value." "Literature," he says, "fed on the sap of economics and a surplus value was necessary so that socialist writers may flourish and produce great works, just as in the labor front in the Soviet the Stakhanov movement was producing more, the workers even taking home work to add more wherewithal, therefore making a material surplus for everyone."

Ma popped her head in from the kitchen to ask "Tom Paine" why the Soviet authorities arrested Isaac Babel, the great Jewish writer, and why he was never heard from again.

"Alexander Hamilton" didn't agree with "Tom Paine" on Stakhanovism. He said that this kind of material surplus wasn't a transition from socialism to communism but a naked and crude speedup at work and a backward imitation of 1910 capitalism.

"Tom Paine" talked about Stalin's guiding principles of socialist realism. He said that socialist literature would revive tragedy and would also revive comedy because the " 'new man' would want to laugh."

My mother came in to pour some tea. She remembered

when my father used to bring some piecework home after a full day of hard work in the shop and how she helped with the sewing and pressing and how they were falling off their feet. She joked about it, asking if that was Stakhanovism.

Molly was gone again. There were no phone calls. She was gone all week, then returned with "Emily Dickinson." They came in dancing the Charleston. . . . They set a new fashion in makeup: shaded eyelids, round pink cheeks, cupid bow lips, and short hair with bangs. My sister Marion said that it looked as if Molly and "Emily Dickinson" went out to get a haircut. Molly changed the subject, turning to my brother "Patrick Henry" sitting next to her. She told him that with the completion of the next five-year plan, the Soviet Union would pass the United States in the production of meat, milk, and eggs.

Albert Laspira, "Alexander Hamilton," showed up at the next meeting dressed in army khaki. He was being charged with Trotskyism and the "woman question." "What do the goddamn women want?" he shrieked. We listen to him say that communism fits the Soviet like a saddle fits a cow. He was charged with being in a conspiratorial group. The others at the meeting sailed into Albert Laspira with a vengeance, that he was a petty opportunist and stooge for the Trotskyites. Albert Laspira, aglow with the glamour and glitter from the dialectic thrashing he'd gotten, was also charged with saying "bitch" in regard to a certain comrade. A week passed. Suddenly it was rumored that Albert Laspira had confessed and had been thrown out of the Party.

Tony, the brother of "Alexander Hamilton," a well-known neighborhood moneylender and tough guy, stood next to his new Packard roadster on Southern Boulevard and spotted me coming out of Miller's Ice Cream Parlor. "Hey, Leon, how come you don't have nothin' to do wit' my brother Albert? He's a 'Troskeeite,' so what? He talks like you guys. So what's a 'Troskeeite'?"

Molly was back again. A week had gone by, a week of uneasiness. Everything pointed to the dissolution of our room. Linen was scattered about the floor, stockings, dresses, slips, panties . . . She came and went without modesty, without shame. She left a note to say that she would be away dancing for a few days.

"Betsy Ross" decided that I was the man to run for Assemblyman in the West Bronx on the American Labor party ticket, but first I had to get fifty thousand signatures to get on the ballot. After a month of bell ringing and canvassing, we were set to go. Night was approaching. I saw a glowing purple sun setting between the buildings and on the opposite side a bright, shining pale moon rising. It seemed as if I were seeing such a sunset for the first time. I was atop the sound truck. Nobody had showed up from the Labor party. The police were supposed to protect me, but they stayed a block away, deciding we were "commies," as did the driver of the sound truck, who took off saying he wasn't hired to be a bodyguard. He went into a nearby bar. A gang of teenagers showed up and tried to turn over the truck. The truck shook like a ship in a storm. It took a balancing act to keep from going over the side. What held me together was my amplified voice bouncing off the nearby buildings. "Friends, my name is 'Paul Revere,' and as I speak here tonight I speak about opening a second front in Europe to defeat the Nazi armies in Normandy."

Things began to get bad at home. Molly threatened if I didn't move out of my mother's house, she would go live with "Ralph Waldo Emerson," a neighborhood accountant. A few days later I found Ma in bitter tears, pointing to my missing furniture in our bedroom. Molly had left and taken the bed, dresser, several suitcases, and my Little Lenin Library: *State and Revolution, Infantile Disorder,* and *Lenin in October.* "Susan B. Anthony" called to say they were going to bring me up on charges on the woman question plus social chauvinism.

The United States had entered the war and I wound up in the Navy. Three years later I was discharged at Pier 92. The house I lived in on Undercliff Avenue was high on a bluff overlooking the Harlem River and the nearby woodland. The sun was shining and the only one waiting for me at home was my dear old Ma.

A Lazofsky

◇

April 12

I take Ma out of the Home for the day. She's wearing a hat
with a wide brim and a gauze veil to protect her skin from
the sun. We are dressed up—I am in a striped summer
suit with a shirt and tie—and Ma walks to my car in full
step, highly motivated. We are going to visit my brother
Ronald, in Teaneck, New Jersey.

Ronald finds Ma doesn't communicate well anymore.
His wife, Doris, says, "Let's face it—Ma isn't getting any
younger." Ma is eighty-nine. She sits quietly for a minute, then asks if we remember Harold Tanney. We remember the name—the son of a friend of Ma's.

"Harold Tanney's wife, Hortense," says Ma, "brought
home her poor old mother, who is ill and needs careful
watching, so Harold Tanney gave up his place in bed and

sleeps in the hallway, while his wife, Hortense, sleeps with her poor old mother."

"Harold Tanney has to be out of his mind," says Doris.

April 17
Ma begs me, implores me, to take her back to her old apartment: "Just for a little while, Leon."

I try to convince her that the old neighborhood is completely finished, that there isn't a sound brick in the whole block, that there is nothing left in her part of the Bronx but rubbish and rot. She stands in the doorway of her room waving good-bye. I wave back. Distress passes over her face something awful.

May 6
The social worker tells me that Ma's been washing towels in the toilet bowl. I mention it to Ma, but she's not listening. She's thinking back to a time fifty years ago.

"When there was no food in the house, I made do with the scrapings from the bread box and we managed a whole month. When vegetables were in season, I did them up in mixtures. With chopped onions, carrots, turnips, and even peas I could make any kind of stew. We ate all week."

On my way out of Ma's room, a door opened along the narrow passageway, and a man in a dressing gown imparted a message to Ma that the menu at the dinner table was gefilte fish appetizer, barley soup, chicken with potato pancakes, and homemade honey cake. "Just so you shouldn't leave the table hungry, missus."

May 13

Ma wears a silver-fox fur piece and a white kettle hat. We are driving to visit Ronald and Doris again. Ma's vitality is fantastic today—absolutely marvelous. Doris has prepared a chicken dinner, and during the meal, Ma is amused by her own image in a soupspoon: "Who is that person, Leon?"

After we eat, we go into the living room and I tell Ronald and Doris that Ma remembers Slobodka in 1910 and that each time the details get better. I ask her to tell us about her hometown.

"In Slobodka . . . there were barnyard noises . . . roosters . . . cows . . . and sheep. . . . When it rained . . . the dusty roads were deep in mud. . . . My family had a small garden in the back . . . for vegetables. . . . On the right . . . a narrow pathway led to an old tower. . . . In back . . . to the left . . . on the same road . . . you can get to the wooden synagogue . . . and then . . . the wooden houses . . . one by one in a crooked row. In the last house lives a man, Lazofsky, in his fifties. . . . Married with two children . . . Zlota, a girl, twelve . . . and Ruven, a boy of eight. His wife, Hannah, is five years older than Lazofsky."

Doris yawns. "Lazofsky?" she says. "What's a Lazofsky?"

Ma smiles. "Hazel," she says, "I'm not so dumb. You'd never guess that I breast-fed little Ronald—and what a fine, fat, pink baby he was." Ma is mixing up Doris again with my brother's first wife.

"It's not Hazel," says Ronald. "It's Doris, Ma. Doris."

I suggest to Ronald that Ma stay at his place for a week or two, that the change might do her a great deal of good. Doris complains that she doesn't care for a change. Ronald puts his feet up on the table. He lets out a deep sigh. He is wearing slippers embroidered with kittens running around the sides. He sits there at his ease, as his hi-fi plays Handel's "Sarabande."

May 21

I get a phone call from the Home that Ma is "sinking." I'm in tears as I drive out there, thinking of Ma and the old days. When I arrive, she is feeling better and walking around a bit. I tell her that I was singing "Barney Google" on my way over, and she says, "Meshuggener, you're a scatterbrain and always was one."

June 3

Ma enjoys going out to the diner today. She doesn't walk—she seems to gravitate. Feeding her has become a circus act of knife, fork, spoon, open, chew, swallow. People at the other tables enjoy watching; we have become diner celebrities.

I remind Ma of a famous meal from years ago: "Remember old Cohn?"

"That bandit!" Ma had met Cohn, a widower, on a bench at the lion house in the Bronx Zoo. Cohn had changed his mind about marriage and asked Ma for her hand. Our flat quickly filled up with widows; some came to meet Cohn, some to steal him away.

"How come you asked all those women to the house, Ma?" I say.

"When the widows saw how much he ate, they lost their appetite for him. He swallowed everything." Ma says she had prepared delicatessen—pastrami and corned beef, young pickles stiff and springy, and a half-dozen "specials." Cohn struck the dish with his knife and attacked the first "special," sticking the fork into it as it quivered, red and pink. Extending his tongue to meet it halfway, he bit it, shaking his head and ripping at pieces of rye bread. Coleslaw and potato salad with the bread, back and forth, old Cohn's eyes rolling into his head to watch his swallows going down. . . .

"What happened to the marriage, Ma?"

Ma shrugs. "Old Cohn disappeared the same way he came. Winter was over and he was back in the Bronx Zoo, where he belonged."

I am astonished by Ma's recall of that meal.

June 10

The way Ronald was lounging around when Ma and I came in, I thought he had forgotten us. He was sitting at the wide-open window, looking at the sky through a telescope. He had a dazed, dreamy expression and didn't like being disturbed. "See the stars in the Belt of Orion? They look like they're heading over to join the Seven Sisters. You see, Leon, I could have spotted Betelgeuse myself."

The meal consists of sardines, sesame wheat, and cucumber soup. Ronald and Doris are on a strict diet. Ma likes chicken and is disappointed with Doris's menu. She complains that she is lost in America. Doris ahs and bahs about senility resulting from old age, often accompanied by marked deterioration. Doris was a surgical nurse in former years.

I suggest to Ronald that we go look for a good nursing home for Ma up around Hurleyville, in the Catskills. "The country life! That's for Ma! Open spaces, forests— poultry and chickens, if you will."

Doris is disturbed. "Leon," she says, "did you notice

that Ronald looks lost in his old clothes? Especially his pants, which have nothing to hold onto he's gotten so thin." I try returning to the subject of Ma's future in the country, but Ronald puts another record on the machine and adds sternly, "Albinoni's Adagio."

June 20

When no one comes to the Home to see Ma, she sits alone in her armchair, gazing at the wall. I've come in quietly. Spotting me, she says, "Where did everybody go?" She wants to visit with my family and maybe stay a few weeks.

I bring her home, but it's not like the old days. My wife Sally and I and our two sons come and go. Ma feels neglected. At dinnertime I have to fetch her from her room. She says Sally doesn't want her. I bring her a brandy and she comes out. She doesn't care for our cat, Myrtle, and says its nose is too large. Myrtle is very friendly, hoping for some of the chicken Ma is eating. Ma talks to Myrtle in Yiddish and gives her a piece of drumstick. My wife reminds me how her late father had gone to work well into his eighties and then, when he was taken ill, "had no place to lay his head." I remind her that back then we had only four rooms, that our two sons were in one bedroom, that my studio was in our bedroom next to the fire escape, and that the only place for her father would have been on my lap at my desk.

June 30

Cousin Ben, a correspondent and columnist for a Jewish daily, bounces into the Home today. He goes quickly from office to office, making a gesture with his thumb and index finger—the "OK" sign from the fifties Ballantine-beer ads. The administrators at the Home know Ben and welcome him with handshakes, hoping for publicity articles and pretending that Ma is special.

Ben and I go up to Ma's room. Her nurse, Mrs. Caplan, a comely woman of forty or so, comes in, and Ma asks if she's married or single. Mrs. Caplan says, "Occupied, my dear." So Ma asks Ben if he'd like to meet a nice social worker. Cousin Ben, a bachelor in his sixties, has been left high and dry without personal family, and has become a "goody," visiting Ma at the Home with uneven frequency. Ma has never figured how Cousin Ben stays unmarried after all these years, especially since his newspaper job includes the Bintel Brief column of advice to the lovelorn. "Dear Editor, We're two sisters in love with the same man. Our names are S. and G., and we're smitten with a boy who's deceived both of us."

Ben and I take Ma out for a drive into the city, and on a side street in the East Village I see a couple in a loving embrace on top of a station wagon. I don't have my watch, so I stop the car, lean out of the window, and ask them for the right time.

When we drive off, Ben explodes in a tirade. He says to Ma that my head's not screwed on right. "The insolence of it! Your behavior," he tells me, "is unbelievable. You're capable of anything—a cataract of base instincts."

Ben is wearing a celluloid collar that he's been using for years to save on shirt and laundry costs, washing the finger and sweat marks with a sponge.

July 9
I go into the dispensary with Ma for her weekly checkup. Dr. Steinberg is almost as old as Ma. He moves slowly

and like an automaton. First he goes around his desk once or twice, then he goes around again. Ma says her trouble is insomnia.

The doctor applies the stethoscope. "There's nothing to worry about," he says, as if addressing a crowd far in the distance. He climbs up a ladder to the cabinet where he keeps his samples. He suggests pills from every shelf: "There's something for every disorder, for every obsession."

Back in her room, Ma says, "Listen to me, Leon. Gingold passed away and Mrs. Kelly passed away and Mrs. Siegel passed away only this summer. All the old people sitting on the benches fell over one by one this year."

"Passed away, Ma? A person dies. Nobody passes away."

"You're all alike," Ma says.

August 1

Ma doesn't walk in the garden, because there's no one to walk with. She makes friends at the Home, but they don't last. She says she's all skin and bones.

I assure her that she doesn't look as bad to others as she does to herself. "You have the face of a girl, Ma. Even your hair glows. How is it to be old, Ma?"

Ma explains that age means knowing she'll never feel perfectly well again, never move easily or hear or see well. She speaks of family life as it was before the Second World War. "Our neighborhood had plenty of old people. In those days families lived together—grandma, grandpa, aunts, parents, children, all in one apartment."

I tell Ma that more and more, as I look into the mirror, it's her face looking out at me. My sister Marion has nice ears. Ronald and I have European ears. Some of our uncles have bat ears. A donkey or two.

August 10
"Well, bust my shocks . . . this is Big Monroe, good buddy . . . swattin' flies and kickin' tires. . . ."

Ma and I have come down to Miami to visit Marion and her husband, Monroe. He's got a citizens-band radio in his Cadillac and talks road tough. I've come here with a plan. If Ma could stay at Marion's over the summer, she would have a grand vacation and get out of the Home. I could break up Ma's time with visits to my house. It would spark Ronald, and I might slip Ma under his door. But I can't help bad-mouthing Miami, and say I'd never live here because the water table is running out. Marion and Monroe don't like to hear that, and I never get my plan for Ma on track.

"Up the hills an' down the dales . . . haulin' chickens in my flatbed . . ." *Poulet crémaillère.* Monroe is picking up all the restaurant tabs, using credit cards by the score, inserting them everywhere, pulling out money from cracks in the wall. I don't care for the million-dollar homes sitting on top of each other, and say so.

"Smokey on my tail . . . cuttin' fog in an eighteen-wheeler . . ." There is too much heavenly hash flying around, and I leave with Ma, without accomplishing my mission.

September 10
It's Ma's ninetieth birthday, and we've all come together at my house. Marion is dressed in leopard. "Ma was so

vital," she says. "It was only yesterday she was so together, so darling." She is holding Ma's head with both hands. "Dear Ma, you're so peaceful, so beautiful." Marion bursts into tears. "Ma doesn't even know who I am anymore!"

Cousin Ben raises his wineglass in a toast to "Drezzle"—Ma's nickname from the Old Country. "You know, my mother used to say that Tante Drezzle was quite a girl on the other side. A classic beauty. Unbelievable how she spoke on the telephone. And to this day her voice comes in steady, controlled, regular." Ben counsels, "This is not a day for old family animosities. It is, in fact, an opportunity for bolstering family pride. All of us can see that Drezzle's feeling better, and old sores and feelings of guilt and remorse for any real or fancied neglect can be forgotten."

Ma fixes an eye on Ben and asks him why he hasn't found a suitable girl to settle down with yet. She reminds us about Marion's old beaux: "Herbie, Willie, Harry . . ." I ask Ma if she recollects a Mr. Abrams, in children's dresses, from 1930.

"Who, Abrams? That lecher!" Ma had met Mr. Abrams at a lodge affair, and she might have married him except that she made the mistake of asking a Mrs. Silverman, also a widow, up to meet him. "He nearly fainted from her perfume. It made him dizzy. And who cooked dinner?" Mr. Abrams pinched Mrs. Silverman's cheek in the middle of eating, leaving Ma's face hanging over a bowl of soup untouched.

All of us are startled by Ma's clarity and well-being. She is actually standing. I ask her to tell everyone what kind of fur Pa sewed onto the collars of overcoats when we were kids, and she says, "Kolinsky."

Doris, who has been boiling and bubbling—a mystery—gets up from her chair. "He's instigating!" she hisses. She sinks back and fans herself with a magazine. She puffs and blows her nose. My brother makes signs not to rile her, to keep absolutely quiet, that it will pass. Childe Roland and Kate Crackernuts.

Cousin Ben gets up to leave, and I go with him to the door. "Leon," he says, "we will never forget Drezzle's bright hour tonight." Parson Goodfellow.

When I return, poor Ma is crawling around on all fours. She's come apart again. We help her to the sofa in the living room. Ma is in some kind of stitching process, her hands reaching for invisible threads, busy, undone.

Doris sighs. "If you sleep on the floor, you'll never fall out of bed." Ronald is philosophic: "We must laugh before we are happy, for fear of dying without having laughed at all." Doris is in tears now, sobbing hard. "Ma did her very best until the end." Doris is yammering. I am fascinated. Is she going to turn blue? She huddles against Ronald, once in a while letting out a hiccup.

I butt in and tell them about how I had a phone call only last month that Ma was low and I should come to the Home, drove all the way crying and singing old songs like "You Know You Belong to Somebody Else," and when I got there Ma had recovered and was on the fifth floor having lunch. Ma might bounce back, and I could bring her home again.

December 7
Back at the Home, Ma sits in a wheelchair and doesn't recognize me. She stares as if to say, "Don't ask me anything more."

April 6

I come up to see Ma and sit with her for a half hour. She seems to be thinking. Her eyes have remained sky-blue. Her silence is unending. I take a chance and speak to her: "Ma, remember Cousin Ben? Cousin Ben got married, Ma."

For the first time in months, Ma turns her head toward me and speaks. "Cousin Ben got married? To whom?" Then, almost as though she remembers that she's old, she turns away.

Cousin Lillian

◊

WHENEVER MY AUNT LENA or uncle Albert telephoned from their house on Myrtle Avenue in Brooklyn to our house in the Bronx, one of them would listen in on the extension downstairs in their dry-goods store and my cousin Sonny would pick up the receiver on his bedroom extension. When Sonny telephoned, my aunt would listen from the living-room extension. When my aunt or uncle picked up the phone in the store, the two others listened in on the upstairs extensions.

It was a Friday night and Ma was on the telephone with my aunt Lena. Since Ma was going deaf, we had put in a special telephone, with amplified sound, so that a whisper could be heard all over the house.

"What will become of Lillian? What will become of

her?" my aunt shouted. "She stayed out all night. She didn't come home all night. Who knows where she stayed out all night."

Ma said, "Lillian's talking to Leon right here in the living room, right now. She's been here since yesterday. She says she tried to call home and no one answered. The line must have been off the hook."

My aunt was skeptical. "Off the hook? No one answered? Albert was in the store until ten. Sonny was in his room all night, and I was in the parlor. Sonny was in his room. Albert was in the store."

Ma said that Lillian had slept over at our house. "On the sofa, Lena. I made up the bedding myself."

My aunt shouted, "You're an accomplice, Drezzle! That's right! An accomplice!" My aunt wanted Lillian to confess. If it was a man, my uncle and she would go together and see him. My uncle wouldn't last very long if he kept working himself up about Lillian.

Cousin Sonny, listening from his bedroom extension, said to Ma, "Listen, Tante, that boyfriend Harry who Lillian brought home can't keep out of our kitchen even when Papa's about to eat after all day in the store. The day before yesterday, Tante, while Papa was trying to swallow, Harry had to creep into the kitchen and talk about socialism for cows and chickens. He came at Papa with 'Today's cow and chicken, by Hindu law, may be you and me tomorrow, Mr. Cooper.' "

Cousin Lillian looked out of our living-room window. The light from a streetlamp was on her face. I'd never seen her in a tight-fitting blouse before. Forlorn on our sofa, she listened to Cousin Sonny, whose voice continued to trickle over the telephone. Raising one arm, she said to me, "Leon, Harry was just joking with Papa." Lillian leaned toward me to whisper. "Leon, I first met

Harry in group therapy. He and Dora shared a room and were beginning to work out their problems when Dora left Harry for Bernard, also in group therapy. Harry came home and found an empty house and realized at once that Bernard had been studying his personality—even the way he used to say 'Let's face it' to Dora all the time. All of a sudden Bernard was saying 'Let's face it' to Dora, smiling where Harry never smiled. Leon, Harry was left with a split personality. He could joke with Papa, but when we were alone he called me Dora. . . ." Ma moved nearer to us with the telephone to pick up what Lillian was saying. "Leon, when we were in bed he was totally with Dora. He wanted me to move in with him without a license until we were sure it was us."

"Dora's in bed?" my uncle muttered from the extension in the store. "Who's Dora?"

From his room extension Cousin Sonny commented, "Free love. That's the new Party line."

"Dora is Dora and Lillian is someone else," Ma said, trying to smooth things over.

"Lillian's getting a license? What for?" asked my aunt.

"No, Lena," said Ma, "it's when she's sure she's not Dora that they'll get a license."

From the sofa, Cousin Lillian frowned at Ma's oversimplification. "I would have lived with Harry without a license but he was always eating, like a nervous tic. Papa caught him at the refrigerator and said, 'What?'—the only word he ever said to Harry. Then last week Harry ate Papa's whitefish and joked about it. 'I left you the eyes, Mr. Cooper.' Then Harry took Papa's wine. 'To wash down the whitefish, Mr. Cooper,' he said. Then Mama got good and mad at Harry and turned on the radio full blast every time he started to say something.

Harry's trauma came back and he started to call me Dora again."

The telephone rang, and Ma said, "Lena?"

"Hello, Drezzle," said my aunt.

Sonny said, "Hello, Tante."

"Hello, Sonny."

My uncle said, "Hello, Drezzle."

"Lillian didn't come home last night, Drezzle," my aunt said. "She's there in your house, and we hold you responsible." She made a hullabaloo about people who were a half step away from the poorhouse. My aunt knew how to make comparisons, to draw inferences. "Albert and I never owed a cent, and we never bought on the installment plan. Max left you with three small children, left you in desperate need. You were left without a piece of bread, with debts at the grocery store and the butcher's, and the month's rent unpaid."

"Don't aggravate yourself, Lena," said Ma. "Lillian just came in through the door with a young man with eyeglasses. A student, maybe."

Cousin Lillian had entered the living room enmeshed in a new boyfriend. Hugging and kissing, they crossed the floor in a cloud of talcum powder. It was hard to see where he began or what he looked like, they were so busy rubbing and caressing. A bird of passion, he pecked make-believe seeds out of Cousin Lillian's lips, puckered in love.

"Charles is an accountant, Tante," Cousin Lillian said.

"Does he make a living?" my aunt asked over the telephone. "What does he do for a living?"

"He's a certified public accountant with a college degree," Ma assured her.

"A certified public accountant?" my uncle asked unbelievingly, slurping from a plate of soup down in the store.

"From City College, I'll bet," said Cousin Sonny in a smirking voice. "City College certified public accountants are a dime a dozen. Accountants are being replaced one-two-three. . . . An engineer, I could figure. Most accountants are going into business for themselves so they can do their own books."

"Charles is a junior executive!" Lillian shouted in the direction of Ma's phone. "Charles works at Columbia Pictures and makes out very well!"

"Accountants," Cousin Sonny continued, "are interested in one thing. Sex. Their work is monotonous. It's bookkeepers and clerks and particularly the certified public accountant that can most afford to hang around after work."

A customer must have come into the store—I could hear my uncle knocking on the ceiling with the broom, shouting to Aunt Lena that he had a customer at the underwear counter.

Sonny ran down to cover for him and finish what he was saying on the store phone. "You went to City College, didn't you, Charles?" he shouted.

Charles said, "Yes. And I'm an accountant. Why?"

"And isn't your last name Franklin?"

"Yes, my last name's Franklin. How did you know?"

"And, Charles, didn't you get a divorce last year, and isn't your present wife's name Mary? And aren't you paying for the upkeep of two kids from your first marriage? And weren't you popular with the pinko lefties at City College?"

It seemed unlikely that my uncle and aunt could have burned with passion in the making of Cousin Sonny. Yet there must have been some consummation—a possessed

Uncle Albert babbling like an approaching Myrtle Avenue train, an ejaculation of socks and ties, winter and summer underwear, children's garments, brassieres and bloomers and stray customers.

Cousin Lillian, wearing a dress of sky-blue silk with splashes of violet, wandered about our house singing songs of love in the Piaf manner:

> ". . . and yet deep in his eyes
> something magic lingered,
> a speck of blue skies . . ."

"Leon," she said, "I met Eugene at the Modern Museum. He said, 'I know just what Kandinsky had in mind.' And that's how we met. Eugene stands very erect and belongs to the Run Two Hundred Miles a Year Club at the YMCA. Eugene is sixty-three, Leon. Six years older than Papa. We're very much in love, and Eugene acts half Papa's age at least."

Ma was pointing the telephone receiver at Cousin Lillian.

"Kandinsky?" My uncle was boiling. "She's going with someone sixty-three? Why not with someone ninety? Yesterday a certified public accountant—today Kandinsky, sixty-three!"

Lillian continued: "Eugene makes a good living playing sax with a jazz group."

"Sex!" hissed Aunt Lena.

"Not sex," Ma corrected. "He plays the sax, Lillian said."

"Ha, Drezzle, you've been deceiving me. You're as big a liar as she is. All week we've been waiting for her—"

Ma said, "Lena, a person ought never to interfere in the affairs of the heart."

My aunt was bellowing so loud we could hardly hear each other in the living room. In the store my uncle raised a terrible clatter on the ceiling with the broom handle. Cousin Sonny ran down.

Dressed in a white piqué frock with lace trimmings, Cousin Lillian reminisced about one of her recent boyfriends, Carl. "Leon, Carl only wanted Papa to place business-opportunity ads with him in *The New York Times*. 'Men with capital wanted' type of ads. That was all Carl meant—to place ads together. He approached Papa at the wrong time. Just when Papa was coming to eat. 'Do you know anything about mutual funds, Mr. Cooper?' he asked, trying to communicate. You know how it is when no one talks, Leon. Papa was always hostile. Remember when we were children, we had to bathe in one tub of water and Papa went around the house shutting off the electric lights to teach us a lesson. He never kissed us when we were little. Except Sonny. Papa didn't kiss him either, but he lifted him up sometimes and said, 'Sonny boy.' "

My uncle seemed about to explode over the telephone. We could hear him pounding the table, something falling over onto the floor and scattering, Uncle tangled up in the telephone wire.

Ma put in a word. "Albert," she soothed, "everything will settle. Soon you'll have grandchildren running about."

"What's that? What's that?" my aunt flung at Ma. "I don't follow you. What's that you say? What's that you're telling us? Who brought relatives over from Europe?

Albert did. Everybody came in rags. We ourselves worked from six in the morning. Drezzle, we saw families being put out on the sidewalks. In our case we had absolutely no one in America."

It was an early spring on our sofa, and Cousin Lillian wore a large red hat topped with optimistic tangerines, happy grapes, and smiling leaves. A little stuffed bird, perched off center, chirped silently in the best of all possible worlds.

"Drezzle, what's going on there?" asked my aunt.

Cousin Lillian came in with Daniel. "He loves me, Leon." She straightened her hat, her dress, and her gloves, then led him onto the sofa, where he folded into sleep with one eye open. "He's tired, Leon," she said, trembling, rubbing her nose in his ear.

"What did she say? Who is Daniel? Why is he so tired?"

Phil was a tall man in a blue turtleneck sweater. Lillian wore a tight green satin dress trimmed with feathers. Her face, powdered chalk white, made a sharp contrast with her black hair, loosely brushed back from her forehead.

From the dry-goods-store phone my uncle asked, "Who came in, Drezzle?" My aunt and Sonny echoed on their extensions, "Who came in?"

Ma said, "Lillian is here with a nice young man in trade-union work."

A burly, impetuous athlete, Phil wouldn't lie still on the sofa. "Herbert Hoover was responsible for my father's unemployment during the Great Depression, so I told them, 'I won't sign a Happy Birthday, Herbert Hoover petition and you can't make me.' So I was the first one laid off in our shop."

Standing on a chair, Phil did an exercise, going up and down on one leg while explaining the woman question. "One, two . . . the women's revolution demands concentration. Three, four . . . it cannot tolerate orgiastic conditions such as are normal for the heroes and heroines . . . five, six . . . of a Henry Miller. Seven, eight . . . women are a rising class. Nine, ten . . . they don't need intoxication . . . eleven, twelve . . . as a narcotic or stimulus. . . ."

"What do you mean, like Henry Miller?" the magnetic Cousin Sonny piped in from his bedroom extension.

"Thirteen, fourteen . . . self-control is not slavery, not even in sex." Finished with one leg, Phil lay down on the floor "to let blood into the head." Then he went on. "Left opportunism is always ready to destroy women's as well as workers' revolutions, to smash the machinery of the bourgeoisie, leaving nothing to produce wherewithal with, therefore making it possible for the return of exploitation and capitalism."

Cousin Sonny asked, "If all the money was divided, then what?"

"Without wherewithal, there is no bread," Phil said. "Now push-ups."

Cousin Lillian said, "Phil was clubbed on the head twice by company police during the textile strike in Raleigh last year, Leon. He's a very militant trade unionist."

"The rehabilitation of the ruble and the five-year plans proved once and for all how important wherewithal was."

Cousin Sonny repeated, "If all the money was divided, then what?"

"After push-ups, deep breathing. The . . . petty . . .

bourgeoisie . . . is . . . the . . . handmaiden . . . of . . .
reactionary . . . capitalism. . . . The . . . leaders . . . of
. . . the . . . women's . . . revolution . . . that . . . have . . .
middle . . . class . . . orientation . . . will . . . sell . . . their
. . . interests . . . and . . . become . . . the . . . watchdogs
. . . of private . . . property. . . . Now sit-ups, for stomach control."

"Why do I have to divide a savings account with anyone?" persisted Cousin Sonny. "What's mine is yours,
and what's yours is yours, right?"

"Kerensky was swept away by the tide of history. Social Democratic leaders never change their class spots.
They talk revolution, yet under the whiplash of the boss
they smile and wag their tails. . . . Now I do this for
concentration." Fixing his head on the floor, he lifted his
legs and stood upside down, facing Ma and the telephone.
"The small storekeeper is finished forever, caught in the
nutcracker of history."

Cousin Lillian beamed. "Tante," she announced, "Phil
and I got married yesterday."

Uncle ran up and Tante ran down. Sonny ran out of the
house, and a Myrtle Avenue train passed over their heads
on the uptown side.

Hortense

◇

ORTENSE FLUTTERED into Miller's Ice Cream Parlor in a fur jacket and jade earrings. A friend at our table assured me that her jacket "is definitely mink," her earrings "are worth at least a couple of hundred dollars"— and "her father drives a Pierce-Arrow." Hortense sat herself down at our table. She said, *"Je suis Parisienne, et voilà!"* She was studying French at James Monroe High School. I told her that I was in my last year at DeWitt Clinton High, the all-boys school in the West Bronx. She didn't like my hair parted in the middle, so she combed it straight back, pompadour style. I wanted to bring her up to my family's apartment, but we didn't have a real living room. Ma and my sister Marion used it for a bedroom.

My brother Ronald and I slept in an adjacent room, and the room near the kitchen was for boarders.

When Ma first hung a BOARDER WANTED sign outside the entrance to our building, a Mrs. Bodner and her sixteen-year-old son, Bernard, came up and asked to see the room. Mrs. Bodner, a woman of about fifty, bent and wrinkled, looked down at the floor as she spoke, asking the price and were there kitchen privileges. They agreed to ten dollars a month, and Ma gave them the third shelf in our icebox. Mrs. Bodner reached into a shopping bag, took out a newspaper-wrapped herring, and placed it on the third shelf. By the end of the week Mrs. Bodner hadn't paid the ten dollars' rent. Ma discovered that they had been eating into our food. Our cheese was gone, and five eggs had disappeared. Ma caught Mrs. Bodner and Bernard in the kitchen eating our chicken. She demanded an explanation. Mrs. Bodner denied having taken our food, opening the icebox and pointing at her shelf. Ma pulled out the newspaper-wrapped herring and opened it. There was no herring inside! Ma insisted they leave in the morning. "It's them or us," she said.

Ma was selling dry goods and novelty jewelry to old friends, neighbors, and relatives, on the installment plan. She ran herself ragged, loaded down like a mule, looking all over the city for new and overdue customers. I tried selling light bulbs from house to house. One day I combed Tremont Avenue near Southern Boulevard. At my ring they would open the door a crack, and when I said, "Any light bulbs today?" they would slam the door in my face. I tried the small businessmen who were dozing through the Depression in dimly lighted storefronts, who hadn't sold anything in days. They didn't even answer when I said, "Any light bulbs, sir?"

Back home, seeing my mother's distress, I started in again. "Light up your life, madam. Two bulbs for forty cents."

Hortense lived with her parents in a new apartment house with cutout corner windows, on the Grand Concourse at 174 Street. A doorman let me in and buzzed her apartment. There were several large chandeliers hanging in the lobby. A plastic strip of rose garden separated the blue carpeting from the red-paneled walls, and a pair of large matador paintings flanked the elevator. The elevator man let me off on the sixth floor. Hortense introduced me to her mother and father, Mr. and Mrs. Beecher. Mr. Beecher was a tall, lean, gray-haired man in silver-rimmed eyeglasses. He asked me if I drank or smoked, and I told him I didn't. Mrs. Beecher had light-gray eyes, somewhat protuberant, and soft mouse-brown hair in a bun on each side of her head. A pianola in their sunken living room was tinkling "Dew Dew Dewy Day."

Mr. Beecher told me that President Roosevelt was ruining the country with giveaways and boondoggles. "They don't want to work!" he declared, tapping me on the chest. "They dig a hole and fill it up again. There are breadlines today paid for by people who want to work and do. Life is tough. Only the strong survive. The weak fall by the wayside." Then Mr. Beecher said he and his wife expected Hortense to be home by midnight.

I tried to wind up this date with Hortense at Miller's Ice Cream Parlor, but she was in the mood for Chinese. We went to Hung Fat, on Southern Boulevard—a waiter-and-tablecloth restaurant with big squarely folded napkins. Hortense ordered Heavenly Chicken, and something called Loong-Ha Peen for me. Halfway through the meal the waiter brought us finger bowls, tepid water with a few flower petals floating on top. There were two or three underlings to service us, going back and forth.

I got a summer job, working in the basement of the Katz Bakery. Eleven dollars a week; up at three A.M., through at noon. I loved the roll machine. I would throw a large lump of dough into this giant crisscrossed iron pan, then pull a lever and bring down the heavy top. It capped the dough, squashing it into small units, each enough for one roll.

Mr. Katz, the baker, and his wife, Sarah, a petite, matronly brunette, spoke strangely to each other. She would bounce down from the kitchen upstairs and shout at Mr. Katz in four-letter words: "Listen, you _____, you can eat _____ if you don't get that damn strudel on the _____ counter by ten o'clock." Mr. Katz laughed ecstatically, overjoyed at her verve and devotion. "Listen to her!"

When the bakery had its annual cleanup of bugs, mice, and rats, several barrels were filled and put out on the sidewalk. There were roaches in dark corners, scurrying about as big as mice. "These roaches," I said, "are bigger than mice! And when I step on one, it doesn't crush and my foot moves with it!" Mr. Katz laughed at my fright. "Listen to him!"

Mrs. Klingman was our next boarder. We called her the Lady from the Park, as Ma had first met her on the benches near the camel house in the Bronx Zoo. A large woman of fifty or so, she had bristly steel-wool hair and eyebrows that arched, giving her a look of astonishment. She cooked up a storm, using all four fires on our gas range at a time. Her pots overflowed. She'd stay in the john an hour, and took to lying around on our sofa, smelling of lilac, making eyes at my brother Ronald and calling him Cousin. Ma was afraid to leave the house.

When I told Hortense we took in boarders, she said she had never heard anything like that before. *"Je désire une chambre à un lit avec salle de bain."*

Hortense and I had been alone in her house all evening. At her least smile, waves of magic ran through me. I was afraid to look at her. What moved me most was the charm that lit up her face when she spoke. She turned on the radio:

> *"Au revoir,* a fond cheerio,
> a bit of tweet tweet . . .
> Yowsah, yowsah, yowsah."

Oh, God! I couldn't stand Ben Bernie! I turned the Beechers' radio dial and got Edgar Bergen and his dummy, Charlie, on NBC. Just then, Hortense's parents came in. They had been to a banquet and were all dressed up. As Mrs. Beecher removed her fur cape, I noticed a string of black pearls that fell nearly to her waist. I had never seen black pearls before.

Hortense was rumored to have an uncle in Newport who was a millionaire with a racing stable, a summer house, and several limousines, and dressed for eight-course dinners. Once, she had shown me an ornamental ring her uncle gave her on her sixteenth birthday. "It's a real sapphire centered in a diamond hexagon," she had whispered.

Seeing me ogle Mrs. Beecher's black pearls, Mr. Beecher laughed. "Diamonds, *too*," he declared, "are a woman's weakness. No matter who the woman or what her position in life, she will have a soft spot in her heart for those precious stones."

I got a new job, at a dress factory on West Thirty-seventh Street, at twelve dollars a week. The factory was a large room with a big red-hot stove to keep the pressing irons ready for use. I was the delivery boy and had to wear this damn cap that said DAISEY FROCKS. There was a wooden fence, waist high, separating the finishers from the cutters. The boss, Mr. Margolis, decided to get rid of it, so I spent a day chopping and sawing, full of splinters. Mr. Margolis liked how I worked, and said I had a future at Daisey Frocks. They were starting a new line in girls' dresses, and he said if I showed willingness, after a few months maybe he'd send me out on the road with a salesman to carry the sample cases. I'd get to know the customers up close, he promised.

Mr. Margolis had a partner, Mr. Cohn, who heard me say, "A month is just another day on a dumb job," so he fired me. Mr. Margolis asked where I was going, and I told him I'd just been canned. "Come with me," he said, so I got taken back and was fired again later in the day by Mr. Cohn for lingering and wasting time holding a door open for a delivery man coming in with a large bundle.

"Stupendous! Spectacular! Sensational!" At the entrance to the Bug House a giant mechanical head with rolling baby-blue egg eyes, one large lid opening and closing in conspiratorial winks, said, "Wanna hear a good one? Someone asks me do I like bathing beauties. I don't know—I never bathed one. Ha-ha-ha-ha. Wanna hear a good one? . . . Ha-ha-ha-ha . . ."

Hortense and I passed a pitchman at the entrance to a large tent with some kind of auction going on inside. "There goes a lady with another of those ten-dollar watches! Hold it up, please, madame, so everybody can see it! I'll level with you, ladies and gentlemen—these beautiful watches are not worth fifty dollars each, but they are a tremendous bargain at one dollar apiece! . . . There goes another gentleman with a genuine leather wallet with one single dollar bill tucked away in it! Hold it up, sir. Thank you. We are now going to give away ten of the finest, ten of the biggest, ten of the costliest gifts for the price of five dollars each to the ten lucky people with an ounce of sporting blood in their veins. . . ." I bought a five-dollar ladies' fountain pen for Hortense and a one-dollar wallet for myself.

We rode the Caterpillar. We were jostled and bounced and thrown into each other's laps. Hortense got dizzy from the Roulette Wheel, so I did the Human Pool Table by myself, getting flung from disc to disc. Hortense had an hourglass figure, and I encouraged her to enter the Steeplechase Park beauty contest, but she said she wasn't ready. "I've got a face full of freckles," she explained, "and I'm keeping out of the sun this summer." She did have vanilla-malted skin with a smash of freckles on each cheek. *"Qui veut la fin veut les moyens."*

We hung out the BOARDER WANTED sign again, and a Mr. Perez came up and rented the room for ten dollars a month. A dark man with an Adolphe Menjou mustache and a perpetual twitch, he tailored fashionable men's suits for Macy's and other department stores. Ma tried to get an extra dollar a month from him for all the electricity he used with his sewing machine. He worked day and night, then dressed up in one of the new suits and wore it in front of the house for a few days before delivering it.

I had been wanting Hortense to meet Ma and the family, and one day as we approached the house Mr. Perez seemed to be having a fit at the entrance. He was slapping his arms about in a new tweed suit, trying to rid himself of cockroaches that had settled in his pockets and were crawling around on his person. Some neighbors standing there acted astounded, as though ours were the only apartment with bugs in it. I decided not to bring Hortense up, and passed Mr. Perez, pretending that I didn't know him, that I didn't live there anyhow. That I wasn't me.

One night I had a date with Hortense and it was pouring. Bronx Park was hopeless, but I only had two dollars on me. I suggested we go to the Belmont Theatre, on Tremont Avenue, to see *The Power and the Glory,* with Spencer Tracy, but Hortense wanted to catch the acts at the Loew's Paradise Theatre, on the Grand Concourse. "Every nook and cranny in the theater is filled with regal museum furnishings," she said.

"For the best remaining seats, ladies and gentlemen, take the grand staircase on the left." We stopped for a moment to watch the ceremony for the changing of the ushers. There were fifteen daytime ushers in royal-blue uniforms surrendering their flashlights to fifteen evening ushers in white tie and gold-braided West Point jackets.

The head usher marched them down among the Renaissance columns in the lobby, where he read them their orders. He then put them through a close-order drill, marching them into the theater and to their posts. "Left, right, left, right . . ." I figured that they got about eighteen dollars a week—the head usher maybe twenty-five. I wondered out loud whether they had to pay for their uniforms themselves. Hortense didn't care. We sat in the balcony, and she nudged me. "It's so lovely to look up and see the stars twinkle."

I reminded Hortense that the stars would be turned off when we left the Paradise.

My next boss, Mr. Barish, said, "People are fed up with slobbering salesmen. In New York you can't get away with it. The main thing is to come forward and speak when the customer asks for something, to hold your tongue until you're spoken to. I'll try to inform you, but before taking any risks, I'll have to see what you are good for. If you're competent. If you're cut out for the job. If you're loyal. And you'd better get this straight: if you're not up to it, I, myself, will fire you personally."

I dusted his hardware and swept up twice a day. What was terrible was the silence, the endless time waiting for a stray customer, and Mr. Barish sitting behind the counter looking straight ahead. I worried about how he could pay me at the end of the week, since he took in nothing. I swept up again.

Finally, after two weeks, he turned his head toward me. He had discovered the worst symptoms in me, he said. He washed his hands of me. His conscience was clear. "Leon," he said, "out of consideration for your mother, I am not going to dismiss you." (Ma sold his wife dry goods occasionally.) "Your mother is taking you back of her own free will. You see the difference? Believe me, I'm sorry to see you leaving us. But at your age, you can always make up for lost time." He shook my hand with a great deal of conviction.

My last suit was sagging every which way, with large bags at the knees. My shoes were worn. Ma said I didn't walk like other people. She was still waiting for things to pick up. She had hope that hand-knit sweaters would come back in style, that the taste for handicraft would return. She was wearing herself out for nothing. Her customers had lost all refinement, all appreciation for handmade articles. All they had left was an infatuation with machine-manufactured garbage.

I bought a tin lizzie for forty dollars. It was a stick shift, and I learned to make the *H* backward and forward. I convinced Ma that I could drive her around to make her dry-goods deliveries to customers left and right.

Hortense's cousin, Shirley, lived in Bridgeport, and I offered to drive her there. Mr. Beecher wanted us back by midnight. Thirty minutes out on Boston Post Road we had a flat tire. I put the spare on the car and let the jack down. The spare was flat, too. Hortense said, *"Pardon, monsieur, où est le train à Bridgeport, s'il vous plaît?"* Then she suggested that we look for some water to test the leak; as fortune would have it, we weren't too far from a brook. We submerged the tube, and with the rising bubbles we found the hole. The damn tube was already full of old patches. I added one more. A hand pump came with the lizzie, and I pumped too much air into the tire. As we drove off, we could feel every bump and lump on the spare. I decided we'd better get a new tire, so we stopped at a garage and I borrowed ten dollars from Hortense, adding my five. Twenty minutes later we developed a knock in the motor, followed very quickly by a belch of black smoke up front. The crankcase dropped onto the road, spilling bolts and nuts and oil. We got back home at two in the morning.

Hortense's father was in front of their house waiting for her. I had oil smears all over my shirt and pants. I let her father babble awhile. I didn't know what to say. I was listening with only half an ear.

I spotted Ma on 180 Street, leaning against a mailbox, resting her bundle on the ground. She looked thin and sallow, and she was all wrinkled around the eyes. Ma's dry-goods business was sinking beyond rescue. Even at rock-bottom prices she couldn't sell anything more. Her customers were stone-broke. She hadn't even kept her books accurately. She had several "ledgers" in different drawers around the house, and wherever she happened to be, in one room or another, she pulled open the nearest drawer and entered a payment. We weren't sure who owed us what.

"If you're not on the ball, you won't eat," Mr. Beecher said. "Anyone who wants to work can get work." He had decided to give me a job at Ajax Valves. He thought me a little large for his shop. Even without me in it, no one could move about in that mess. "You want to join us. Fine. It's settled. Splendid! Shake on it. We understand each other. Good. Welcome aboard."

I got twelve dollars a week, nine of which I turned over to Ma. It was a fast job—back and forth into the stockroom, carrying boxes of valves, pins, and discs. I never waited for the elevator. I ran up all seven flights. I got coffee for the boss and the foreman. I swept up. It was impossible to lay hands on the right parts. I'd grope for some washers on a shelf and start an avalanche of small bouncing springs. At the press machine, punching valves, I'd take a disc about the size of a quarter and place a five-inch pin through a hole in its center, then push a rubber washer onto the pin against the disc, then slip a metal spring onto the pin. Another washer, another disc. I placed this assemblage on the press and, holding it tightly, stamped it together with my foot on a lever. My fingers got mashed. I mixed up parts. When I showed the foreman, Felix, the bent pins, crushed together with discs, washers, and springs, he couldn't believe his eyes. He looked me up and down. "Let this be a lesson to you," he said. "What little you've learned here will surely be of use to you somewhere else."

An ARTISTS WANTED ad in the *Bronx Home News* brought me to Klassy Ties, at Lafontaine Avenue and 180 Street. I had some samples from my high-school magazine, and a variety of drawings I'd done over the years. It was a free-lance proposition: Klassy Ties wanted nude figures of women hand-painted on men's ties, at fifty cents a tie. I tried it for a week, but I was too slow, and my figures were too knobby.

I answered another ARTISTS WANTED ad—Landscapes, Inc. The head artist showed me the job. He laid out twelve eighteen-by-twenty-six-inch pieces of black plush extended on wooden stretchers on a long table. "They will all be of the same scene," he said. He moved quickly along the table, painting the moons first; then he did a medieval castle on a lake, twelve times; then trees and swans on each. He was very fast and finished the twelve paintings in an hour.

I was assigned to do a dozen paintings of a sunset in the Swiss Alps, with chalets and several milkmaids and cows dispersed all around, at four dollars a picture. I was thinking that Ma's customers might be interested, as this sort of painting was already appearing on the walls of many homes. I myself had seen a balcony scene of Romeo and Juliet on black plush in Hortense's house.

At the Bronx River boathouse, I hired a boat, and Hortense and I rowed upstream. Bronx Lake was full of late-summer sounds, with hidden crickets and a close-up sprinkling of fireflies and mosquitoes. We floated into the shadows along the far bank. "Leon! Leon!" she whispered. The boat was shaking. Her whole weight came down on me. She clutched me. She sobbed into my ear. I was flattened under her caresses. I kissed her, and she cried out, "Oh, you've kissed me!" She broke loose and jumped back, almost overturning the boat. We got to her house on the Grand Concourse at three A.M. The doorman said Hortense's father was thinking of going for the police. The next day there was a special-delivery letter from her, saying that her parents had forbidden her to see me again. "So I think it best that you don't write or phone. *Je regrette*—Hortense."

Mr. Novak, the art director of the poster-art department at Fox Film Company, was a handsome man with a high-bridged nose and flared nostrils. He rose to greet me, and looked at my drawings. He liked my work and said he'd seen dozens of portfolios and was going to give me a job, though it might take a few weeks to get me on the payroll. Two weeks passed, and all of us at home were waiting to hear from Gerry Novak.

Ma said that he was probably one of those film mogul's sons, a mental, who's given an office and whoever comes by gets a job.

"Yes," Marion added, "and Gerry Novak was sick when he was a kid and wasn't allowed to eat solids at the gloomy old parsonage while the rain beat off the moors onto the windows. . . ."

Ronald had to put his two cents into it. "Yes, and a strange, uncanny atmosphere broods over Gerry Novak's office, where the sun never shines and bedbugs crawl about. . . ."

In the meantime I was painting signs. Two cow heads in burnt sienna and Prussian blue—one cow head at each end of the sign, which was five feet by ten feet and read KAPLAN'S KOSHER MEAT MARKET. Mr. Eckle, of Eckle Signs, did the lettering. He enjoyed my cows and said they had sex appeal. We had another sign to paint, on the side of a building, with a big herring by me across the center, for Levy's Appetizing—a twelve-dollar-a-week job, and in the neighborhood. I had plenty of time to think about sex appeal up on the ladder.

The doorman said he had seen Hortense go into her building about a half hour earlier and she hadn't come out again. At her door, I knocked softly. I knocked again, but no one answered. I knocked louder, and at last her mother opened the door. She didn't seem glad to see me. She said that Hortense was out, that she couldn't be sure when she'd be back, that she'd gone up to her girlfriend in the country. Hortense's mother didn't ask me to sit down. I saw her catch someone's eye in the living room, as if giving a sign, and I got a fleeting glimpse in the foyer mirror of Hortense close against the wall.

During my lunch hour I telephoned Gerry Novak for the fifth time, and he asked me to come down to see him. I wore one of Ronald's old suits, and my shoes were polished fit to kill. I barely had time to dash in to see my boss, Mr. Eckle, and drop off his paint box. He wished me the best of luck. Downtown, Gerry Novak told me that I was on the payroll as an apprentice for thirty dollars a week! My brain whirled.

When I got home, the family was sitting down for supper. I asked Ma how much I'd get for myself if the job paid twenty dollars a week. She said five dollars.

"And if the job pays twenty-five dollars a week?"

"Twenty-five dollars?" she said. "Leon, at twenty-five dollars you keep eight dollars for yourself."

"And if I'm paid thirty dollars, Ma?"

"Thirty dollars!"

We danced around the table, exchanging kisses, embracing, and marveling at the miracle of the money and the "art job." Gerry Novak had become a heavenly body. Marion asked me if he was a laughing and a joking man, ruddy-complexioned, a picture of strength and happiness.

"Yes, Leon," Ma said. "Yes, Leon." She kept repeating it to herself, looking off into space.

That Friday I got my first paycheck and cashed it. I needed some clothes—maybe a Harris Tweed suit, some sweaters, a few shirts. I'd never been to the Catskills. Maybe I'd spend a week of my vacation at Sorkin's Hotel, in White Lake.

I denied Hortense's existence, yet I actually carried her

photograph around in my pocket. It was a snapshot of her with hands on hips, chin tossed high, laughing at someone over her shoulder, who was outside the photo. Maybe her father thought I was on a lousy twelve-dollar job running a freight elevator.

As I was about to go down the steps of the subway entrance, a man in a Happy Hooligan coat buttoned all the way down to the sidewalk caught my eye. With a hand up to his mouth he whispered, "Hey, kid, you wanna buy a hot diamond ring for ten dollars?" He proceeded to prove it was a real diamond by cutting into the glass pane of the adjacent United Cigar store window. There was a cut in the glass, all right, and I was convinced. I gave him the money, and he handed me the ring. I hurried over to Forty-seventh Street and stepped into a jewelry shop to price my bargain. I was told the ring was worth approximately seventy-five cents.

A Midsummer
Night's Dream

◊

MY FRIEND MARIO had a closetful of frayed, moth-eaten wigs, capes, and high hats that he had swiped from the Butler Davenport Free Theatre, where he appeared weekends as a spear carrier in *King Lear*. During the week, he and I were busy acting out scenes at home. We did assorted Gothic shtick, lighting candles and using other spook paraphernalia for *Dracula*. ("Velcome to my kessle. Come freely, go safely, and leave someting of the heppiness you bring.") With pale-green greasepaint on his face, bushy paste-on eyebrows, and plastic pointed teeth protruding over his lower lip, Mario did Dracula crawling out of the window and down the fire escape headfirst, his Davenport cape spreading out around him like great wings. Mrs. Goldberg, on the floor below, popped her head out of her window in shock, calling, "Leon! Mario! Are you meshugge or something?" Meanwhile I did Jonathan Harker in full voice: "What manner of creature is this in the semblance of man? I feel the dread of this horrible place."

Soon Mario and I began leaking out onto the street with our theater. Wearing a Davenport wig, cotton under my upper lip, and a marble in each nostril, I stood in front of Beberman's Bakery, glowering at the gorgeous cake in the window. It didn't take long for Mrs. Beberman to come out with a sizable slice of strudel. "Mister, eat a piece of cake and go home to bed."

Mario and I made our way down to the boathouse on the Bronx River. Dressed in an outsize suit and a Davenport wig, I stood in front of a number of people who were seated on the benches. I blurted out, "To hell with Hitler!" And "God couldn't be all over the place at once, so He made mothers!" And "If I were hanging from the highest tree, I know whose tears would come up to me— my mother's."

The spectators warmed up to my declarations, saying, "May you have long years" and "A blessing on your head, mister."

Carried away, I shouted, "Here's to us all! God bless us every one!"

I said, "Missus, it's only a short time since your wedding and already you've trampled your husband under your feet."

There were cries of approval and laughter from the crowd. "Not bad." "Listen to what he's saying."

Mario wisecracked that I was ugly enough to stop a clock. In one jump, I was on top of him. He went over under the impact. People on the benches slid away. Mario got up and took off. That was the Stanislavsky method.

An old man came over to me and asked, "Mister, you don't feel good? Mister, rest a little. Where do you live, mister?"

My sister said that it seemed like an awful lot of work for Mario and me to go down to the Bronx River and upset everyone just to get dates.

At the Free Theatre, Mario had been promoted to the part of the Fool to Mr. Davenport's Lear, king of Britain. Mario argued with Butler Davenport that Lear was an idiot who deserved what he got, having given away everything he owned to two of his daughters, who then threw him out, leaving him bellyaching in the rain without a place to sleep. Davenport answered that *Lear* was the most powerful of the Bard's tragedies. Mario noted that the Fool got the best of it: " 'Nuncle; thou hast pared thy wit o' both sides, and left nothing i' the middle.' " I cautioned Mario to be discreet or we'd be out of wigs.

I finished a plate of ziti at Mario's house. I was in my second year of Italian at school, so I thanked his mother in Italian: "*Tante grazie,* Signora Petrello. Your ziti was great."

She smiled, saying, "*Ogni bel gioco dura poco,*" which meant "All good things come to an end."

Everything was ethnic where we grew up. "Dirty wop," "Lousy kike," "Mick bastard" were everyday street talk. It wasn't always easy to get to Bronx Park. One Saturday afternoon we ran into four guys on the street. They got around us, and the biggest one of them couldn't believe Mario and his beard. He kept baiting Mario: "Hit me. Go ahead—take the first punch, Jewboy." This guy was big and mean, with a face like a horse. Mario hit him. The guy folded up on the sidewalk. His friends helped him up and took off with him. We walked silently for a couple of minutes. Then Mario said that the guy he had hit was Tybalt, nephew of Lady Capulet.

Love that river! The *Pride of the Bronx,* a small launch, was chugging its way upstream, full of people, making waves that hit both banks. It was the first week in July, and Mario and I were out for more "natural theater." Mario thought we could build up our acts and maybe land a job in the Catskills the next summer as social directors, for fifteen dollars a week with room and board. Good-bye, hello!

We walked around to the benches by the boathouse and faced an audience who had come out of their apartments to escape the heat.

"Ladies and gentlemen," I announced, "we are going to give a performance well worthy of your attention. The talented young Mario, from the Butler Davenport Free Theatre, is now going to do his famous Needle Act."

Mario stood there in a red wig parted in the middle, looking at the audience with a hundred odd twitches and many unaccountable absurdities on his face. I had already started laughing. Mario bowed to the crowd. He then squatted, pretending to be a tailor, wetting a nonthread with his lips, trying to thread a make-believe needle—a hit-or-miss business, full of grimaces and head cocking. Then came the sewing. In a frenzy of stitching, he sewed one hand to his leg. As he pulled on the needle, the threaded hand followed the pull. He then sewed his leg to his head, and his head to his other leg. Held together by thread, he finally passed the needle into one ear and out the other, sending the crowd into bursts of laughter.

Later that day, we took out a rowboat and rowed up the river to Fordham Road, a mile away. The water lay placid, a sheet of green-blue, slightly ruffled by a gentle breeze. After a while dark clouds rolled overhead, and in the air was the oppressive sense of thunder. We were hit with a wind and pelting rain. We were rowing against the current and didn't have time to reach the shore. Stuck in some water lilies, we lost an oar. Mario said that what we were doing with "natural theater" was in accord with Stanislavsky's dislike for the classical method of acting. We bumped into another rowboat, also stuck in the water lilies, with two sisters in it—Vivian and Cynthia. They were dressed in old, long, loose black dresses and had lost both their oars in their struggle with the storm. They, like us, were soaked to the skin. The sisters recognized us from the boathouse.

Cynthia said, "All honor to the first actors of the Bronx Zoo."

Mario told them that soon they would have to pay if they wanted to see us—that they would have to stand on their heads for tickets.

The boathouse had been eating up our material at a rapid rate, so we decided to try a different section of the park. Mario had borrowed two plumed helmets and two foils from the Free Theatre. They weren't exactly foils—they were schiavone, cavalry swords that had ARME DES ES-

CLAVES, GARDES DE DOGES DE VENISE engraved in tiny print on the ornate handles. On our way to the park, we passed a ground-floor doorbell. The temptation was too great. I pushed the bell, and we kept walking. The door flew open, and out came a person in an underwear top, covered with muscles and tattoos. I had time for a quick read of one of his arms: MOTHER OF MINE under a purple heart in a bed of roses.

"You guys ring the doorbell?" He looked at Mario, who stood there in a plumed helmet, with a putty nose and a false mustache and beard, wearing a sword. Without any effort Tattoo Man lifted Mario off the sidewalk by his elbows.

I pulled Mario loose from his grip and said I was the one who had done it and was sorry. "Mister," I asked, "haven't you ever had the feeling that you wanted to ring a doorbell?" I wasn't paying attention to his rage. My eyes were on three kids jumping rope and some birds of summer in the branches of a tree. Tattoo Man belted me on the side of the head, and my knees sagged. Mario stepped in and punched him. Muscles, tattoos, and all, he ran back into his house.

A woman came out, took one look at us, and threatened to call the police. Mario and I began to duel with the schiavone. We raised a tremendous din, clanging the swords together.

"When the little whippoorwills call . . ." One of my sister's beaux, a Sidney Gurvitch, brought her a present of a radio with a horn attachment. The old horn radios were being replaced by single-unit cabinets. Anyhow, the tubes were missing from this one, so it didn't work;

Mario and I took it over for our "natural theater." Mario hid behind a bush with the bottom of the horn in his mouth. I turned the dial on the set and brought in the "programs."

"Ladies and gentlemen, this is Ted Lewis. . . . Is everybody happy? . . . Yeah . . . just Mollie and me . . ."

I turned the dial and got Bing Crosby: "It was a luck-y A-pril shower . . ."

Some wise guys passing threw a half-eaten sandwich into the horn. I wound up with a black eye. Mario took me to his house, where his father applied a leech to the swelling. Mr. Petrello was a leech importer and had these repulsive blue-black worms from Italy packed in green tins in his basement. While waiting for the leech to balloon, we talked about clocks and watches.

"*Che cosa indica l'ora in un orlogio?*" I said.

Mr. Petrello replied, "*Le due lancette indicano l'ora sul quadrante dell'orlogio.*"

Then Mr. Petrello removed the bloated leech with a pluck, leaving a dot of blood under my eye.

At the Free Theatre, Butler Davenport criticized Mario: "If you are going toward a door, you say, 'I am going through that door.' Whiskers and putty noses aren't enough. Dear boy, you have an awful way of flinging your hands about, which I detest."

Mario felt like punching him in the nose.

One night my girlfriend, Kathleen, and I went to the stone pavilion in Bronx Park. It was used for a rain shelter and for dancing on weekends, but this was a week night, and the air was calm and mild. Three of my sister's girl-friends had found husbands there. We had been inside about ten minutes when Kathleen suddenly whispered, "Leon, there's someone standing behind that post."

I laughed. "When the clock strikes midnight, all the evil things in the world will have full sway in the Bronx woods." The words were hardly out of my mouth when I saw a head pulling back into the dark. I said, "OK, Kathleen, let's get out of here." We were just outside the pavilion when this creature ran toward us. He came right up to me, his lips drawn tight in a scowl, his lower teeth showing. A Bela Lugosi look-alike! Another man lingered in the shadows several feet away. I said to myself, That must be Renfield.

"What were you two doing in there?" Lugosi asked, flashing his coat open to show us a fake police badge pinned inside.

I said, "Nothing special . . . talking things over . . . chewing the fat . . . nothing really out of the ordinary."

Lugosi shoved his face even closer. "Who is she?"

"My girlfriend," I answered. "Luckily we've saved a little money to settle down with. Once I get a job, we'll move to a different part of the park and give ourselves a change of air." To Kathleen I said, "It's only momentary. It will die down in a week or two." I gave her arm a yank. "Run, Kathleen!"

Lugosi turned his head as Kathleen lurched and ran. I hit him on the jaw, and he fell into a shrub. Renfield hadn't come over to help him. Lugosi pulled something out of his pocket. Extending his arm, he pointed the object at me. Of all the wonderful things that had happened that night, this was the worst. I thought I was going to get shot. Kathleen's legs had given out, and she was down in the grass. I ran past her and had to turn back to help her up. Lugosi and Renfield made dangerous sounds but never came after us.

The next time I saw Mario, I told him about my experience in the park. He thought it was a great scenario. He would play Bela's role, and I would be myself. Mario spoke to Butler Davenport about putting it on at the Free Theatre, but Butler Davenport torpedoed it, saying, "It's been done. Boy meets girl. Boy loses girl. Boy gets girl."

The sun was up. There was the snuff mill, the river, and the marsh. There were birch trees in the green of the marsh, and there were snakes. I had seen them slithering about in the tall grass near the shore. I brought a five-gallon can and caught nine two-foot garter snakes. My prize was a five-foot blacksnake sunning itself on a flat rock, digesting something. I placed a stick behind the snake's head and pressed down, and the snake curled around it. Then I shook the stick into the can, and the sluggish snake slipped in. I capped the can with newspaper and carried it over to Mario's house. We hid it in the basement. Our plan was to spill the snakes near the benches by the boathouse to regain the attention of the crowd.

The next morning I went to call for Mario. I ran into his father in front of the house, and saluted him with a short "*Buon giorno,* Signor Petrello." Mr. Petrello passed me by in silence. Then Mario told me that his father had gone down to the basement the night before and, turning on the light, had found the place acrawl with snakes. The first thought that had gone through his head was that a shipment of leeches had somehow grown into serpents.

I suggested to Mario that we write a science-fiction

piece where leeches develop into anacondas and swallow all the members of a family.

That very evening, we set the snakes free near the boathouse. The sight of all those wriggling snakes shocked the people sitting on the benches and set them up for our scene from Sean O'Casey's *Juno and the Paycock*. Mario played Captain Jack Boyle and I played Mrs. Juno Boyle.

ME: Sit down here, Captain.
MARIO: What about?
ME: Close the door there and sit down here.
MARIO: More trouble in Ireland is it?
ME: It's about Mary.
MARIO: Well, what about Mary?
ME: A great deal wrong with her.
MARIO: It's not consumption is it?
ME: No . . . It's not consumption. . . . It's far worse.

A man got up to leave.

"Hey, mister," I shouted, "don't go away. I want to forget you exactly as you are. Mister, let's see your birth certificate for proof you're alive."

The crowd roared at such gems. Someone on the benches fed me an insult: "You should study to be a bone specialist—you have the head for it."

From this I really poured it on. "Mister, you should be careful not to let your mind wander. It's too weak to be let out alone."

One man explained me as a tragic figure. "This person," he said, "is eminently civilized and sane, and possesses a complete logic on the way to survive today's troubles. He is very young and extremely intelligent, but something has gone wrong in his personal life."

A pretty girl from Honeywell Avenue described my antics as "knockabout" and in a long tradition of crowd-gathering buffoonery from the sixteenth century. She said I was a Punchinello.

Suddenly one of her girlfriends ran up, exclaiming that there was an honest-to-goodness real nut trying to kill himself near the waterfall, threatening to jump into the river. We all ran about fifty yards downstream. During my banter with the audience, Mario had wandered away from the benches, and there he was, squatting on a stone wall that was part of the ruin of an old sawmill extending out over the water.

"Ladies and gentlemen," he said, "I appear before you for the last time. I need not assure you of the sad regret with which I say it, but sickness and infirmity have come upon me."

Mario stood up, his knees shaking and every feature convulsed as he stood swaying before the crowd. Tears were running down his cheeks. A man in the crowd argued seriously that it was very disturbing for people always to be hanging or drowning themselves in public places instead of killing themselves privately at home.

"My death," Mario continued, "sets a seal on the fact that I never existed."

A woman, her eyes flashing, offered to take Mario home with her for a good dinner, but Mario waved her off. He then made the sign of the cross and jumped into the water. It was two feet deep. When we removed our disguises, we were surrounded by a sea of friendship.

When I next saw Mario, he told me that he'd been thrown out of the Free Theatre by Butler Davenport himself. Butler Davenport, playing Claudius, king of Denmark, in the last scene of *Hamlet,* called out, "Give them the foils, young Osric." Mario, as young Osric, had to hand the foils to Laertes and Hamlet so they could duel. Mario withheld the foils, and Butler Davenport called again and again, "Give them the foils, young Osric! Give them the goddam foils, young Osric! . . ."

Freight Train

◇

THE FREIGHT TRAIN came in fast and I hopped onto one of the passing ladders of one of the first cars. I climbed up only to discover that Mario hadn't made his jump on time as the freight had picked up speed. It was a hundred-car job and I ran along the catwalk from one car to another looking for Mario. He had grabbed onto one of the freights down the line and had been running toward the front end looking for me. We met finally on one of the middle cars.

We were riding the Nickel Plate railroad in the flatlands of Indiana going toward Chicago. There were a lot of us riding the top of the freights going West looking for fruit-picking jobs. Mario and I worried about sleeping up on top what with the lurching and turning and the fear that we might tumble off, so we used our knapsack straps, hooking them to the catwalk. How safe can you get? Mario talked about himself becoming a boxer. He knew what a left jab was and what a hook was. He licked some pretty fair neighborhood kids and we'd had a lot of street fights back in the Bronx where we lived. Mario was eighteen and I was two years younger.

This guy with a limp came along with just a shirt on his back and sat down next to us on the catwalk. He spoke about his troubles; he had worked on heavy equipment. "My leg was broken," he said. "It had been crushed and it never mended properly. Now I'm trying to feed my family at farm work. I wasn't in the habit of being pushed around. The thing about my family is that we never had to depend on someone else for our livelihood."

The blowing wind brought a chill and I was sorry for the stranger and offered to share my blanket. But during the night he rolled up and wound himself in the whole of it. I yanked some of it back but he was fast asleep and I felt the cold all night. Mario had tucked himself in tight and had been asleep for hours.

The train let go an earsplitting shriek and I felt a shiver run through me. I was thinking of Mrs. Feldman's daughter back home on Honeywell Avenue and of her father in his room and how he was bound to wake up and find me there. Certainly not on top of a freight train. The tumult and clangor of the train yards in Fort Wayne coming off the sidings into the nearby mills, the switching and the coupling of the cars . . . Mammy! We were excited for two weeks! We settled in the Fort Wayne yards, lifting cement bags onto boxcars and such. Then they put us on drilling and my hands swelled from the vibrations of the big electric drill. A day later the drill cracked and I took it to the foreman, but he was too busy to give a damn. When Mario cut one of his fingers, we figured out that since neither of us was married we didn't have to work that hard or at such a great speed, even though we were getting the job down pretty good and the boss was going to offer us steady work. Then again, we might get to like it out here and stay. So we quit.

Mario and I were in an empty one-hauler freight, trying to doze, passing through sleeping towns and out into the woods again. We got off near Kenosha, Wisconsin, and did some truck farming for a Mr. Wilber, picking and sorting tomatoes and packing them into crates piled up in rows. We were all tuckered out after a day's work of bending and stooping. Mario bet me that I couldn't hop over one of the top crates. I leaped up, catching my sneaker on an edge of a protruding crate, scattering and squashing tomatoes all over the ground. Mr. Wilber's battered face had seen all kinds of weather but he'd never seen anything like this! He laced into us raving and sputtering, making a terrible hullabaloo. He took two days' pay from us, gave us our share, and fired us. "Get out and don't come back!" he barked. Mario said, "Up yours!" And we were gone.

The train squealed out of a hole under some old red houses and became elevated for a while. We were in an open freight with a load of sheep. We didn't talk much, as there was so much maaing and baaing going on. We even got used to the smell. Mario said he preferred cow shit. A cow was a milk-giving graveyard, and besides we could have been drinking milk as we rode. Mario was right about cows, though, large and milk giving. I said, "At least a bull remains independently individual in its way. What remains of today's cow is an emptiness with a hollow head." Mario said, "The bull is the tough end of a cow and more nearly the way the world is. Fight and die."

I said that my preference was lamb chops, anytime. . . .
And that's how it went all the way into Gibbon, Ne-
braska.

A mile or so outside of Gibbon we got jobs picking
onions, cucumbers, lettuce, carrots, and watermelons for
a week. Mario loved the watermelons, using them for
weight lifting, building up his biceps. The farmer we
worked for told us that if we got a good crop, that was
more or less our reward: "You don't work by the hour out
here," he said. He paid us a few dollars each day and
spoke to us as though we had a great career going. "I'll be
happy to have you work on the farm on one condition, if
you can deal honestly in a day's work. Just a handshake,
we won't need a contract." "What contract? The hell with
that," Mario said, and we walked right off the farm and
kept walking.

We're on a Great Northern freight with the clickety-
clack, clickety-clack of the wheels. Mario is shadowbox-
ing and jumping rope. I'm talking with this guy who got
on a few miles past Denver, going west toward California. He spoke with a kind of drawl. "We didn't own our
farm. We rented it. It was a small farm; we only kept two
or three cows, enough to have our milk and butter. We
raised chickens, in fact, raised everything we ate. A
farmer can't live like, say, a dentist. Break the dollar
down and the farmer's at the bottom of the pile with the
smallest slice." Mario was explaining what kind of training he was into. "I get up in the morning after seven
o'clock and run around three or four miles, go home, take
a shower; by nine I'm having breakfast. Then I start
punching a sandbag, one of those handmade things. You
have to have all that stuff to work with to learn how to
punch. You got to be able to fight in close."

I fell asleep thinking of Selma. Selma, who had a

Buster Brown haircut and dark brown eyes. She came into the house on Honeywell Avenue with a piece of candy. I followed her into the bedroom. Her voice was ever so soft and tender. No one had ever spoken to me that way before. My mother and sister were out shopping and my brother was at the public library. Sex? Almost sex.

The diesel chime-horn let go a blast and I was wide-awake, with the thumping of the freight going over crossovers and switches. We were once again out in the country, the sky full of stars and train signals and Selma.

It was raining when we reached Laramie. We asked a passing cop where we could sleep for the night. "In the clink, kid," he answered. Mario and I had our own cell in the jailhouse. "A night's lodging," the cop called it. Some of the cellmates didn't like our visit. "Hey, you guys! We gonna kick the shit out of you when we get out!" Mario laughed and said, "You guys'll never get a chance. You're gonna be in here forever and we'll be out in the sunlight after breakfast and you know what we're gonna have to eat? Uccelleti, scoppati, and stuffed clams."

What bothered me most in jail were those creepy cock-roaches crawling around. Mario said they were roasted and eaten in Taiwan: "Just for the protein," he assured me. At nine o'clock the lights went out and we got into bed in an upper and lower. The noises at night filled the dark with endless farting and growling, burping and snoring. There was the harsh bray of air horns from time to time on passing trains. I began to think about my mother and would I ever make a living? In spite of my good intentions it was no cinch landing a job. My mother outfitted me to make me more presentable. I'd gone through my shoes and she bought me a pair with enormous jutting soles so they would last at least two years.

They were awfully misfit and I hobbled along the streets waiting for my feet to grow into the Thom Mcan's.

We left jail the next morning early and got a ride from an interstate truck driver who was going across the Sierra Nevadas. He told us how lonely he got not talking for days and how, on the road, there were no women to kid around with except for waitresses. The weather was still bad. The squalls and storms came bounding across the roadway. The weather cleared and you could see for miles over the countryside. It began to rain again, and this time when it stopped there were bursts of sunshine, soft breezes, and sweet enchanting smells with daisies quivering in every field. The driver let us off at North San Juan, California. I hadn't seen my aunt Jo for a number of years and I decided to pay her a visit. I telephoned her from a nearby grocery and she was overjoyed that Mario and I would be there shortly. We turned into a narrow roadway with the name Strawberry Hill, and after a mile or so we found her house and her dog, Sidney, who was kept on a chain and barked us in. She said I had grown quite a bit and we spoke about my family. Aunt Jo made us some ham and eggs and some milk and told us how her life had been. Her husband, Harry, had deserted her some time ago, and as they never had any children, her life had been very lonesome. "Harry'd left me this house, and yet from time to time he'd lumber in. Once he'd found me with this good friend of mine, Wilson. I had ways of bringing Harry to task. The minute Harry would walk in the door I'd call up Wilson, who lived close by, and he'd hop over and we'd hug and kiss and drive Harry mad. Harry didn't give a damn about me anyway. He was a big man with lots of silver hair and baby-blue eyes, a handsome man, I suppose. He'd arrive and lurch after Wilson and the chase was on, but let's face it, Wilson was a hare and only came to life when people like Harry was after him. Wilson himself had trouble with his own wife at home."

We stayed at Aunt Jo's for a week, and on the last day, she took us up this hill to get a view of the Sierras. On the way we met two dapple-gray horses that trotted up close to us. Aunt Jo said that these sweet stallions, Chester and William, were looking for some cubes of sugar and were the loveliest and gentlest of creatures. Aunt Jo offered them some sugar and they almost thanked us as they turned and ran off. "Isn't it strange," she said, "and how odd that Chester and William became horses instead of people? With horses like that you wouldn't have war anymore and no more capitalism either." I remembered that Aunt Jo and my uncle Harry had been Marxists.

On the way back down the hill, we saw a number of people swinging scythes all over the fields. Aunt Jo said, "It's the whirling of broomsticks." It suddenly began to thunder and lightning and rain began to fall. "It's some witches brewing up a hailstorm." Aunt Jo had a great sense of humor. "They're working on a marijuana patch," she laughed. "They're not hobgoblins. . . ."

The next morning we said our good-byes and got a ride from North San Juan to Boise, Idaho, a full day's ride. We heard the sound of a band and located this big circus tent . . . The True Word of God Tabernacle. Inside they were praying and singing hymns. Mario and I listened to the minister hold forth to a sizable crowd. The way he was waving his arms and beating his breast, he was working himself up into an ecstasy and nothing was going to stop him.

". . . when my grandma died, they would not tell me for many days that she was gone. I sensed something was wrong and asked, 'Where is my grandma?' They replied,

'She is home.' When I ran away they looked for me everywhere; finally my dog picked up the scent and they found me lying across her grave, weeping and chilled through with the cold November winds. For weeks they thought that I would not live. God spared my life. . . ."

Mario and I were invited to have some turkey sandwiches and to sleep over on one of the benches. I dozed off thinking of the Bronx and Mrs. Feldman's daughter Selma and how she got undressed this summer night without her window shade pulled down. The strange mystery of a striptease incognito. Another day I went up to her house; she closed the door and all the locks. We went into the bedroom and I wondered what was going to happen. She laughed. "I'm going to tell your mother . . ." It was like a Punch and Judy show. She hiked up her skirt. I couldn't help laughing; she'd run after me with big sucking kisses. I saw stars. She grabbed me by the ears, calling me "sweet little pig." I came up for air. The whole bed was wobbling.

Early the following day we climbed into this open freight going toward Chicago. Two guys hopped on just as it started to roll. One guy, well-built and muscular, the other long and lean, both of them friends. For some reason the muscular guy began to twist and beat up on the skinny guy. One minute he's knocking this guy's head against the wall, the next he's throwing him down on the floorboard, sitting on top of him and laughing all the time, calling the thin man "piss face" and giving him an unmerciful licking. The wiry man struggled to get the huskier man off himself, but he was knocked down nine times by him! I counted them. Then the tide turned. The lean guy hooked his arm around the strong guy's neck and wouldn't let go. He kept a tight grip on his windpipe and his face was turning blue. That went on for half an hour. The big guy finally kicked the other guy loose, caught his breath for a few minutes, and then really began to beat him up. Mario and I moved over to the opposite end of the car to keep from bumping around with them. I asked Mario if we should stop them, but he said that if we butt in these two guys would stop fighting with each other and turn on us. When the train slowed down they both jumped off.

Mario and I wanted to bring home some money, so we got off the train at Des Moines and got a job at this old-age home nearby. We worked at emptying bedpans and assisted at mealtime in the geriatric floor, helping feed twelve people in the dining room. We did our best. They were always coughing and sneezing, and if we came in to say, "Good morning, boys and girls, and how are we all feeling today?" some of them would spit chewed-up grub on the floor. The "residents" all had white hair and looked pretty much the same . . . the women like hens and the men like Saul Steinberg roosters. We fed them liquid mixtures with a farina mix, using a spoon. We cadenced them into an "Eat, chew, and swallow, your left, your right . . . eat, chew, and swallow, your left, your right," the food dribbling out of their mouths with that faraway look of the distant departing elderly, of hello and good-bye. We worked there for three weeks and made a few hundred dollars each.

I woke to an earsplitting diesel-shriek as we rolled into the outskirts of Chicago. The train was coming to a stop, but there was a sudden commotion up ahead. A yard dick with a gun and two police dogs on a leash chased all of us out of the freight cars into an open field. We hid there until it was safe to come out and sneaked back into the yards and found a freight that was starting to go east toward Jersey City . . . and the Bronx.

We watched the purple-glowing sun setting between the branches of the trees and on the other side a bright, shining pale moon rising.

The Old-Age Home

◇

January 8

Ma and I pass the Burns guards at the entrance of the
Home. They recognize her and speak to her. We are out
for an afternoon stroll. Twice a week she and I pass in and
out—every time I visit. She answers the guards in Yiddish; it doesn't matter that they're Italian. "They know
the kind of woman I am," she says.

"Don't marry Sadie Olkin," Ma advises me as we
stroll past one Bronx walk-up after another. "You have
Sally and the boys to think about, Leon. Sadie Olkin is
eighty-five, and it's indecent and shameful."

Her mood changes as she holds tightly to my arm.
"There's a Committee to Save Lives," she whispers.
"We're a special group. We come naked if someone is
dying and cheer the person back to life."

"Naked, Ma?"

"Yes, undressed. We remind the sick of the old days and how important it is to stay among the living. Nobody dies here who doesn't want to."

At Fordham Road, we double back to the Home. In the lobby, an old woman hurries up to us. Her hair is coal-black. Ma says, "Hello, Sadie Olkin," and we stop as Sadie Olkin embraces me, putting forward her lips to kiss.

"Hello, Drezzle," she says to Ma, who is annoyed at her intrusion. "It can all be explained," she says to me. "Your mother cooks up these nightmares. She works herself up. She sees and hears things. It's just a bad time she's going through." She takes my arm and rubs my leg with hers. I'm ashamed to pull away, so she increases the rubbing. She smells of Chanel No. 5. "Your mother is a good woman," she says, "a little mixed up only."

Ma watches us and begins to talk to herself. "What you've got to realize is my son is a good boy," she says. "It's only the other side of his kind heart. Yes, he's impulsive. But he knows who I am."

Sadie Olkin winks, then shakes her head at me not to rile Ma, to keep absolutely quiet—that it will pass.

Memorial services are conducted in the chapel. Rabbi Bernstein, the chaplain for the Home, is a robust man with pink cheeks and a tiny white beard. Today the service is well attended, and Ma and I listen as Rabbi Bernstein holds forth.

"We here in the Home express our heartfelt sympathy to our beloved member, Harry Cohn, on the loss of his beloved wife, Sophie, who departed from us last Monday, a week ago. Not that which is loved but, rather, that is beautiful which is loved. Amen."

I ask Ma who Sophie was.

"A person," she answers, "like other people."

January 14

Today there is pandemonium in the lobby. An elderly woman has arrived with bedding and two tattered satchels. She says she has no place to go and is looking for food and shelter. No one knows where she came from. The social workers are trying to find a city agency to help her. After all, this is a private Home. Everybody is scurrying around, and the woman continues to weep.

Ma recognizes her as Mrs. Weiss, from the old neighborhood, and says a word to console her. "When the heart is full, missus dear," Ma says, "the eyes overflow."

The woman sobs, and says, "If a person is destined to drown, she will drown in a spoonful of water."

Ma sighs. They stand looking at each other. "When life falls it falls upside down," Ma says.

The police arrive at last. They are large and bumbling. They talk in low voices, following the poor woman's movements with the abstracted gaze one has for people passing when one is in deep conversation, and scrupulously avoid all appearance of observing her.

"It's the police," Ma whispers to me, keeping close against the wall. She has forgotten Mrs. Weiss and thinks they have come for her instead.

A social worker tells me that if they make an exception in this woman's case, thousands of old people will descend on the Home.

January 22

Ma tells me that last night, during dinner, she got up the courage to ask Bronstein at her table if he would be kind enough to take his hands off her orange, which triggered the wild Bronstein to shout at her. "Missus, you should be ashamed of yourself!" Bronstein said, dressing her down in the familiar *du*. "Yes, missus, we know about all the people who borrow money and don't pay back." This in front of a peer group that included Mr. Rubin, who sits at their table. Bronstein's tirade also unleashed a prune-faced woman, a Mrs. Jacobs, who muttered from her table nearby that Ma had knitted on the Sabbath and didn't keep a kosher home. She then stood up to ask Ma in full voice, "Who set fire to the chicken coop at Rifkin's in Hurleyville? Was it your eldest son?"

Now Mr. Rubin consoles Ma—noticing how distraught she still is today. "We are returning to the Middle Ages," he says. "In those times the Jews created another world for themselves, and, living in it, forgot the troubles around them." Mr. Rubin and Ma shake hands, with an invitation to one another to "come visit next week."

Ma is intimidated by Bronstein. She tells me she is afraid he'll have her sent away, or God knows what. "There are known cases," she explains, "where the police, in addition to money, demand payment in the form of a woman's body."

"With profound sorrow we here in the Home extend heartfelt sympathy at the untimely passing of Saul Bronstein, beloved husband of the late Elsie, devoted father of Harry and Albert, grandfather of Mildred and Phillip Bronstein, survived by two nephews, Chucky and William Smith. Many go through life never knowing a great man. . . ."

Ma insists we leave before the rabbi's sermonette is finished. "A great man?" she says. "A wolf loses his hair but not his teeth."

153

"Why did he die?" I ask.

"Because he lived," she says. "And for stealing oranges."

February 12

Ma says her waiter told her he would supply her with extra food on condition that payment be in gold and foreign currency. A fearful uncertainty has overcome her again. As we walk, I ask her why she was thinking of collecting food, and she says she is preparing a hideout in the closet, with enough supplies to last for months.

I tell her, "Ma, get well again and I'll take you out and get you a little house in the country."

Ma says her social worker will not permit her to move her furniture until the rent is paid for August. Then she tells me that she and several others were seized one night and taken to the basement, where they were ordered to pluck feathers. She came upstairs to an empty bed, she says. She also says that the social workers have declared that no potatoes will be served at mealtime because the guests have large hoards hidden away.

Ma's roommate, Mrs. Goldstein, passes by. Ma can no longer stand her. She is a kind and considerate woman in the daytime, but, according to Ma, she gets "crazy" at bedtime. "It's impossible to sleep with her under one roof," Ma says. "She turns colors at night. Blue and yellow. Let her burst with cholera! I think she's going to tear the room to pieces. She pounds the table with both fists. She kicks the furniture! All night, on all fours she barks like a dog. I shut the lights, Leon, and in the dark someone hits me a hard slap in the face. Who else could it have been? I would rather be poisoned with gas than tortured so. In the morning, it's another day. Mrs. Goldstein's all sweetness: 'I hope you'll understand me fully someday, Rose, when I'm not here to defend myself,' she says then. May she rot!"

February 19
Today Ma changed her room and moved in with a Mrs. Abrams, across the hall. She is a small recluse who always reads the Op-Ed page in the *Times* and is all together in her head. In fact, she acts quite superior. Everything Ma does is wrong. Ma hates her already.

Ma is worrying about the furniture again. She says her bureau and chair have been removed by automobile. She calls it a resettlement. She says the social workers are looking for relatives and friends to share her room: "Strangers to put into bed with! The end of the Old Folks Home!"

This evening Ma calls to tell me she has been moved from Mrs. Abrams' room and is back with Mrs. Goldstein, who welcomes her back. " 'Rose, I'm so glad to see you again,' she says. Then, Leon, a door opens at the other end of the corridor and Mrs. Cohn comes out. She is bent and dressed in a black judge's cape. She speaks in a hushed voice. 'I declare open the trial of Rose Mehler,' she says. 'Born in Slobodka, in 1882 September. In the case of a chicken without payment in the Wilkins Avenue Market on March 1923. . . . Also seen knitting near the Lion House in Bronx Park on the Sabbath, the day of rest. . . . Rose Mehler, there are people lying unconscious from hunger. Besides those who are really unconscious, there are those who fall down in a faint every couple of minutes. You hear their screams for help, but when they land at your feet, by you they are plain beggars.' Then, Leon, a social worker comes from behind and seizes Mrs. Cohn by the ankles and drags her away." Ma is pleased and feels that the tables are turning in her favor.

"We here in the congregation and the board of trustees mourn the passing of our deeply beloved Miriam Abrams, who had seen her ninetieth birthday last June. A thoughtful woman . . ."

"You don't need a calendar to die," Ma whispers to me as we leave the chapel. "She always had her head in the Op-Ed," Ma says. Then she turns to me and asks, "What's Op-Ed?"

March 1
Tonight I get into the elevator and bump into Sadie Olkin. "Sadie," I say, "you're really dressed up!" She wears a green chiffon Russian blouse, loose and baggy in front and back, with a touch of sealskin at the ends of the sleeves.

"As long as your teeth are chattering, you know you're alive," she says. The door closes and we are alone. I am caught, flattened out, crushed.

Tonight we mourn the passing of Morris Schapiro, ". . . dear uncle of Shirley Gelb, also survived by nine grandchildren. We will never forget."

I ask Ma if she knew him, and she says, "Morris Schapiro? He wanted me to move in with him and I told him, 'Everywhere it's good, and in my room it's even better.' "

March 15
Ma has been moved up to the infirmary. The woman in the next bed, whom Ma calls the *meydele* ("little girl"), thinks Ma is her mother.

"*Mamele, Mamele,*" the *meydele* says, "what will become of us?" She has decided I am her father and says, "*Tatele,* take me to the toilet; I can't hold it in," and I turn away.

"The *meydele*'s a great comic," Ma says. "She keeps us in stitches all night."

In stitches? Another old woman in the ward, Mrs. Rothman, is a terminal case, with an intravenous bottle in her arm. She is black and blue from a fall, and she blows green bubbles from her nose. Her eyes are open, fixed on the ceiling. A fly lands on her face and walks about.

March 27
Ma and I pass a room full of the very feeble aged. They lie in trays, with guardrails to keep them from tumbling out. Some are diapered and others leak and defecate where they lie. Ma pulls me into the room. "Say hello to Rabinowitz," she says. Rabinowitz is shriveled and diapered. Ma comes up close to stare at him. She calls him "Cousin." There is a rasping sound in his throat. The words won't come out. In the end he gets out a "Drezzle," and Ma and I say good-bye and leave. ("Drezzle" is Ma's nickname from the Old Country.)

"He's very old," she says. "It's a tragedy to lose cousins as you go. Sometimes in the neighborhood I thought I recognized Rabinowitz in the fruit market. And then, no, it wasn't him. Swallowed up. A terrible thing! And being old doesn't help any. Uncles, cousins, aunts you'll never see again. They've all disappeared like dreams. It's all over. The days and people that pass in the street."

In the lobby, Ma and I meet Sadie Olkin, sweeping along the floor in an embroidered skirt, her eyes darting beneath the brim of a large beige felt hat. "Leon, you're a nice boy, I can tell," she says, placing her hands on my chest. The varicose vein on her nose is blue and swollen.

"Leon, my affection for you remains unchanged," she says. There is a gaggle of old women gathering nearby, and this is for their ears. She locks her arms around my neck.

The women begin to mutter. "When will the *prostitutke* take her arms off him already?" one of them says. They can't believe it. They think Sadie Olkin has discovered the secret of life and is working her way backward to younger years.

"Leon, my affection for you remains unchanged," Sadie says again. She is enjoying herself. "You're beginning to understand me, aren't you? Call me Sadie, won't you?"

I call her Sadie, and a moment later Ma and I leave. Ma is livid with rage. "May her tongue fall out," she growls. Then she asks me if my wife, Sally, is hungry, and I reply that she eats more than I do.

April 3
Rabbi Bernstein holds a seder in the main dining room. It is Passover, and they are serving a meal complete with meat, doughballs, and wine. For a brief minute Ma forgets about her trial and the chicken market. The seder is a source of spiritual strength for her.

According to Ma, certain crooks at the Home walk into a room and pilfer articles of clothing and umbrellas. "They knock at the door and say they are from downstairs and have come to fix things up. Sometimes they take a coat off the hanger," she says, "and put it on over their own." She tells me that the porters are taking everything that can be ripped out of her room—even the faucets and washbasins. Floors and furniture are being torn up and burned because there is a shortage of fuel. Ma says her social worker is selling hot water.

"That's a hot one," I say, and both of us break up at my joke.

This evening, Ma is particularly distraught, looking over her shoulder constantly. She lives in terror of deportation and is writing out surrender papers, which seem to be some kind of special permit—a safe-transit pass. She puts each in a different pocket. "This is the tragedy of wives without husbands," she explains. "Left alive, not knowing what they are living for. Alone in the world."

Ma asks about some of her "outside" friends from the old neighborhood. "How is Mrs. Wilson?"

"Gone, Ma."

"And Mrs. Orfinger?"

"Dead, Ma. Last year already."

Ma isn't bothered by their demise and is pleased she has outlived them. "And Mrs. Greenberg?"

"A stroke, Ma."

"And Mrs. O'Brian?"

"Gone, in July."

"She was a good woman. And her husband, Jim, the retired policeman?"

"He's heartbroken, Ma. I was up to see him. He's alone and covered with dust. Very few neighbors come in to see him."

I ask Ma if she's had her trial yet, and she says yes, this very morning.

A trial in the morning? "What was the verdict?"

Looking up, she says, "Guilty."

"And what was the punishment, Ma?"

She looks around and whispers, "Electric chair."

"Electric chair? Where was it done?"

"They gave me the electric chair in Epstein's Candy Store."

"Epstein is taking in customers for the chair? Where does he give it? In the window?"

"In back of the store." She waves a hand.

"Sarah Goldstein, dearly beloved widow of David, beloved mother of Sidney and Hortense, dearest sister of Alice, Nathan, and Benjamin, cherished grandmother. We here in the Home are separated from you for a short time only."

Ma's former roommate, Mrs. Goldstein, died on Tuesday.

May 12

We find Sadie Olkin sitting on the sofa in the anteroom. She's been falling down lately. She is ashamed to see me. "I'm not feeling good," she says. "I only need a little support under the arms. I won't give you much trouble."

I help her up from her comfortable seat, and she says, "I haven't had a good night's sleep in six months. If you want to know, that's the honest truth. My appetite's gone. When I try to hurry, even on foot, I see stars."

Ma nudges me with an elbow, and as we leave she mutters, "Why should I worry? I measured the risks the day I had you!"

At seven o'clock, entertainers appear in the dining room and sing in Yiddish. We sit at tables. Ma is pleased by the show. There are tears in her eyes. Then she tells me that Schwartz's Funeral Parlor has opened a branch in the Home and is offering burial to holders of American Express cards.

Mrs. Liebman is knocking with a soupspoon at our table, shouting, "All are equal in the Home! All are equal!"

The number of thieves is increasing, Ma says. Money is missing. Ma wears Mrs. Rothman's skirt and the *meydele*'s striped jacket and velvet blouse. The *meydele* is wearing the leopard stole and large straw hat my sister Marion left when she came to visit Ma last July. Coxey's Army.

June 6

Ma wrinkles up in tears when she sees me today. "They told me you died," she sobs. She quickly brightens up. She says she has received orders to appear at the central office and declare herself. A chicken has arrived in the mail in her name. There are 716 doctors on her floor and twenty-one patients. The doctors, she says, are all hoping for Medicaid money. Later, after I leave, she walks off her floor, is captured downstairs, and is brought up again.

Ma now has a Chinese nurse, Miss Ling, who helps her on with her coat and hat. Ma looks at herself in the mirror and doesn't like her appearance: "This isn't my face. If they say dead, you're buried."

I reassure her and say, "Ma, you look like Nixon's mother," which breaks up Miss Ling.

"Nixon's mother," she cries, "Nixon's mother!" blazing up in such animated Oriental beauty as she laughs that I am thunderstruck.

Ma and I visit the chapel, where the rabbi prays for Mr. Rubin, who ate at her table in the main dining room: "Morris Rubin, beloved husband of the late Rosalyn, devoted father of Harry and Meyer, brother of Aaron and of Marsha Kline, grandfather of four, great-grandfather of eleven . . ."

Ma says, "He died a week ago Wednesday, at dinner. He fell off his chair with the tablecloth and the dishes, spilling everything."

July 29

I remind Ma of 1926, when Pa was drowned, and she remembers all the way back. She even remembers her grandfather. I ask her to sing and forget her troubles. "Sing 'Ich un di Velt,' " I say, and she does:

> "If all the world did suffer and I
>   alone knew joy,
>   Then would my door be open to give
>   comfort and love.
>   If she would know my joy . . ."

Tonight Sadie Olkin sees me come into the Home with Ma, and comes dancing over to us, all aglitter. There are various paste jewels attached to her bust—pinned-on lizards and crowns, solitaires and brooches in every conceivable arrangement.

Ma says, "Look at her! One day she's dying and the next day she's a chandelier."

Sadie notices Ma and me looking at her jewelry and says, "These beads are tokens of affection."

Ma tells Sadie that Edmund, the man who cleans up on her floor, wants to marry her, but she won't have him. "Now he just stands there doing nothing," she says, "only looking and mopping."

Sadie is momentarily jealous, and Ma and I leave before she recovers.

Later, Ma whispers that the social workers are throwing loaves of bread to the inmates, "because there is extra." And this seems to have altered her mood for the better. She asks me if I paid the rent yet. She wants to resettle and leave the infirmary for good.

September 10

Yesterday Ma washed some towels in the toilet bowl again, flooding the bathroom and the bedroom. Her social worker is alarmed and tells me they may have to move her. Where to, I wonder. To the sixth floor, maybe? The sixth floor is the end of the line. Ma is afraid and calls it "deportation." She is not moved, however.

Today Ma is dressed in quilted trousers, a vest, and a man's overcoat. Together, we watch "I Love Lucy" in the infirmary dining room. She is glad to see me and whispers that there are informers everywhere. "There are informers involved in hundreds of illegal operations," she says. "A ladder is thrown over the wall and smuggling goes on all night."

I ask her what they are taking out.

"Not out," she says. "They're taking goods in. Instead of going through the lobby, they go up the ladder."

October 19

My sister Marion arrived from Florida last Tuesday in a new leopard and a straw hat, ran up to Ma's room, and spent the day in bed with her, talking of bygone days. Ma was very glad to see her and her happiness lingers today when I visit. She has hopes again of leaving the infirmary and making it to the main floor with the "regulars," even though she's very fond of the *meydele*. Ma tells me she met

Milton Schindler at the entrance to the Home. "He was standing with a policeman," she says.

Milton Schindler? I remember his funeral, back in 1952. I remind Ma that he's dead, but she pays no attention to the idea of a dead Milton, though she acknowledges his funeral. "The police have hired him to fill a listening post on the fifth floor," she says. "May he go on crutches."

November 2

Today Ma wants me to go to the district attorney and get a declaration of her victimization. "There is no question," she says, "that this trial is an instigation—an innocent person accused of guilt never committed!" She says the help is taking everything: "They're hurling sacks of sugar, flour, and the like out of windows to thieves below." She lets me in on a secret: "There are orgies in the basement at night."

Ma tells me that she and the *meydele* have been elected to the United States Senate. They have come back from Washington because not enough attention was paid to them.

"Washington, Ma? Really? How can that be?" I say.

"Yes, the Senate. You don't believe me? Look at the *meydele*. Here is a face of someone we know—someone we have met before, someone to trust."

December 8

When I come up to the infirmary to see Ma, she is busy walking about with the *meydele* and a Mrs. Singer, who wears a tattered kolinsky fur down to her ankles. Ma is dressed in men's pajamas—her hair wild and white after a washing—and the *meydele* has a bandage on her head. They are very agitated, and from a distance they remind me of American patriots at Valley Forge.

Mrs. Singer, who wears the long tattered fur coat, is worrying about the Fur Coat Decree, which affects the whole fifth floor. She tells me it is a severe blow to her. She had this fur coat years before she entered the Home. The third deadline to give up the fur is at six o'clock. Many coats have been concealed about the Home. "Fur-coat certificates are being issued in the main office for a fee," she says. When her husband, Sidney, was alive he sustained a rupture, and Mrs. Singer says she had to schlepp him in and out of bed several times a day, and she has never recovered from these exertions.

Mrs. Singer tells Ma she must go to her room and says, "Good Sabbath, Rose," though it's Wednesday, and leaves.

"Mrs. Singer has had a hard life," Ma says, sighing. "A *mames-a-tokhter*" ("A mother's daughter").

The *meydele* has been caught smuggling dresses from other rooms. Ma wears a dress down to her ankles. Ma likes only her roommates. Everyone else is "the enemy." She sits down and joins a group watching television. "What is the news?" she asks, and a Mrs. Goldberg tells her to make up her own news.

We are going out to eat, and I look for Ma's coat in the closet, and hanging there are men's suits and shirts in a mix. I help her on with her coat, which was in the *meydele*'s closet. She asks me if I know what it says on Sholem Aleichem's stone at his grave. I don't know, and she says, "It says, 'Let me be buried among the poor, that their graves may shine on mine and mine on theirs.' "

December 23
Today I remind Ma how we struggled, years ago, after Pa died. And how we often didn't have food in the house, and how in a mood of despair she once threw herself out of the window—making sure it was the fire-escape window. She remembers, and we both laugh. She suddenly thinks of my father's blue serge suit hanging around, forlorn, in the closet after his death. "Where should a suit go by itself?" she muses.

Ma says the *meydele* was visited the night before by the Committee to Save Lives and they asked her to live a little longer. She is very sick, breathing hard, and her face is covered with sweat.

"We here in the Home record with sorrow and regret the demise of Rachel Singer, beloved mother, adored grandmother, and dearest friend . . ."

"Poor woman," Ma says. "She worried about her fur coat as if it was her late husband, Sidney, himself."

January 4
Yesterday the *meydele* died, and Sadie Olkin was moved into the room. Ma is glad to see her. I peel an apple for Ma, who nibbles on it, pleased with the taste. Miss Ling, the nurse, comes in and diapers Sadie Olkin, who is lying naked in the *meydele*'s bed. Sadie Olkin notices me and tells me not to worry. "Your mother is going to be all right," she says.

Ma tells me there are "illegals" in the Home—unregistered patients who manage to eat stray food and double up in bed at night with the regulars. She says nobody knows how many there are.

166

"Who are they?" I ask.

"They are the everyday old, and they are in hiding," she whispers.

Ma asks if Sally is getting enough to eat on the outside. I tell her she's gained weight recently.

"We here in the Home record with deep sadness the passing of our beloved Sadie Olkin, devoted wife of the late Irving, cherished mother of Fanny, dear mother-in-law of Albert."

Mademoiselle
Simone

◇

Dear Ma:

A word about my coming to Paris. It had best be done in a spirit of adventure. Sooner or later I'll get a room with a bath but find that I usually have to compromise on things or else just keep waiting a matter of months till the right combination comes along. I may find a studio with a bath but then have to concede neighborhood, room size, light, or something else. Or I may find a room with bath but with no hot water. Still, having no bath isn't a serious problem, for each arrondissement supports a public bathhouse with an eye to once-a-week bathing. Food is ample and cheap and most important very, very varied. But skimmed milk is scarce.

All my love,
Leon

Dear Ma:

Here I am studying at the Beaux-Arts in Paris with Leguert, a former student of Soutine, that great antibourgeois! It's an excuse for me to do tangles of crazy color, "I don't know what I'm doing" kind of painting. The sky in Paris in the fall is a misty gray and blue. I'm using neutral tones for my palette, browns, sepias, deep ochers, grays, and violets. I'm working in acrylics instead of oils, as they have a water base and dry quickly.

Last week I met Mademoiselle Simone at the Beaux-Arts School and we are in the same atelier. She paints with a thick paste, which seems as if she shovels her colors with a trowel, yet in each instance her painting is precise and clear. She says, "Painting is the sun, the sky, the daylight, still more light and always light." Mademoiselle Simone says that the art world is seething with excitement. She has a boyfriend, Pierre, who is a painter also. He is in a mix toward abstraction in one of those bastard compositions without color formula, a "wild beast." She wants me to swim with Pierre at the piscine in the Seine, as she is curious if an American can outswim him. I took a lifeguard test and passed the special water exercises beginning with jumping into a pool fully clothed, quickly removing the clothes, doing a crawl, and making my way to the "victim," using a kind of side stroke, pulling him out of the water and then resuscitating him. I'm not a particularly good swimmer and am quickly winded. She's made an appointment for us to meet next Tuesday. Why me? Last year at the Galerie Elysée, Pierre had exhibited a nude female plaster cast, life-size, a sort of poor man's George Segal. It is hardly likely that this surrealist pulpy humanoid could compete with the real-live whores of Place Pigalle.

All my love,
Leon

★ ★ ★

Dear Ma:

I rented a studio room on Rue Jacob on the Left Bank with a ceiling eighteen feet high and a northern light. There are mice and a black cat to chase them . . . a cat and mouse in partnership. I asked the proprietor, a Dr. Fournier, where the john was located since it was never mentioned. He shrugged his shoulders, hinting that I could use the outside facilities in the yard that had once been used for stagecoaches during Napoleon's time. He conceded that I could follow the suite of twelve rooms to the house john itself at the tail end of the apartment. It's a hit-and-miss matter since I have to take a roll of toilet paper along with me and often find the door locked in use. The doctor's wife, Madame Fournier, enjoyed my use of the English and French mixture in trying to locate the WC saying, "Ooo la la, monsieur, vous êtes un abstractionist, n'est-ce-pas?" There was a bad night when the light bulb up on the eighteen-foot ceiling wouldn't shut and I kept calling the doctor all night to shut the damned light and all I got was a faint, distant, "Comment?" I didn't know which one of his twelve rooms he was in. That was cubism.

All my love,
Leon

Dear Ma:

When I first arrived here from Orly the streets were so exciting! I stood on the Champs-Elysées for a long time, prancing about and shouting, "It's maddening it's so wild! The streets are crooked, the boulevards are cockeyed, and the architecture is a mix of everything." Paris is a great glorious bastard!

We paint differently, Mademoiselle Simone and I. She's now painting monsters in mystical legends where beautiful women languish in the bosom of luxuriant pastures. She says she is pursuing Pre-Raphaelite art. "It is spectral sex-appeal," she insists. "I, myself, have been in an automobile accident and have had a love affair with the ambulance driver on the way to the hospital." Her most recent work reminds me of those English fairy tales by that great illustrator, H. J. Ford. Mademoiselle Simone is an astonishing woman. An affair with the ambulance driver? That's surrealism!

At the moment I'm painting disciplined disorderliness. Abstraction, free compositions, triangles, and rectangles. The faster I paint, if you would, the better my color and courage. When I am surprised at the quick of it, I'm very pleased.

Mademoiselle Simone's father, Monsieur Legrand, passed us by on the Rue de Lille last week, and there was never a word of greeting. Not a hello or a good-bye as we pass . . . maybe it was my French. Yesterday, while out promenading with Mademoiselle Simone, at the first glimpse of him coming toward us, I took a chance and spoke quickly: "Bonjour, monsieur, comment allez-vous?" *He walked right past me without a sign. A squash of a man with silver-rimmed eyeglasses, a pink, roly-poly, tight, little-lipped monarchist with a pointed beard.*

Mademoiselle Simone smiled. "Papa is introvert, n'est-ce-pas?" *I think of him in yellow ocher and purple for veins and arteries and constipation.*

Love,
Leon

January 18

Dear Ma:
A restaurant I frequent is the Athenée, a Greek joint. Their main feature and spécialité de la maison is dannier kebab, a sort of charcoal-broiled lamb roast that revolves on a spit. This is

171

turned by hand. *The chef, in whites and a three-foot hat, who I'm sure was once a saber instructor in the Greek army, spins it delicately with the point of a four-foot butcher knife. The streets, buildings, and people are all delightful, and I pinch myself every once in a while to see if it's really me here in Paris. My French is improving by leaps and bounds and compared to last year I'm beginning to speak fluently. I still haven't been able to find any skimmed milk.*

Today I spotted M. Legrand walking along Boulevard de L'Admiral Bruix. I walked alongside of him and spoke about art. Since I was going to visit Mademoiselle Simone anyway, I continued along next to him. I could have crossed the boulevard and gone into the Bois and lost him. Instead, I said, "Monsieur, I keep seeing shapes in paint that have figurative sensibilities in them and I continue to wonder why are they there? Where do they come from?" M. Legrand turned suddenly to his left and disappeared into Avenue Raymond Poincaré.

All my love,
Leon

February 4
Dear Ma:
The other day Mademoiselle Simone recited, at school, part of a novella she's writing:

"Yesterday was so sunny I went down to an Italian training ship on the Seine with a 'Visitors Today' sign. Three Italian naval cadets smiled and made signs of safety with fingers on the palm, so I followed them through an opening down a ladder into a room full of stuffed naval heroes. Octavio beckoned me into a cramped passageway with dangling baloneys. Then we went down another ladder into a squeezed lunchroom with a table and bench. Octavio slipped into an opening in the wall and came out

with a big pepperoni which he cut into four eight-inch pieces. After lunch Benito pointed to an opening under the table and made more signs of safety and honor with fingers in the palm. We slid in, one at a time, down a corrugated laundry chute into a clothes basket, down into a laundry closet with a mattress on the floor. . . ."

I said her writing is cubist and she argued that her intention was surrealist. How to explain Mademoiselle Simone, whose talent is so many-sided and so unbridled? She paints as she writes and she writes as she paints. Her sexual fantasies are especially bizarre. Her art is changing, too; if anything it is Dada and antiwar. At her studio she shows me a number of new canvases. Dreams of Rubble, Sex with a Midgetman, Love in an MX Silo, War and Peace, Hydrogen Man, and Napalm Girl. "I worry," she said, "about my grandmother sitting by the window eating a crust of bread and saying her rosary." I ask if she's painting French missiles and she showed me a triptych she was working on about the Mirage, the French bomb that can go from Paris to Moscow. "For the unfortunate people I worry and have heartaches for the orphans and all the victims." We talk about the great age of surrealism and Dada art and that much good painting is still very vital, plus the nuclear question of war or peace . . . a remarkable woman.

> All my love,
> Leon

Dear Ma:

I was interviewing Mademoiselle Simone for Parisienne, an art journal published by the Beaux-Arts. "I was always able to paint," she said, "and never really needed teachers. Smells were generally the things I remember at home. My uncle Phi-

lippe, who was a portrait painter, sometimes used me as a model, and the wonderful smell of the oil paints instilled in me, even as a girl, the desire to become an artist. . . ." While walking on the outskirts of Louveciennes, Mademoiselle Simone claimed that it must be appreciated that the attention paid by poets like the late Apollinaire, Aragon, Breton, and Cocteau to the work of the great painters was largely responsible for the reception the artists received. Our walk became a wild adventure when the rain came down heavy and wet. The tempest was so violent that Mademoiselle Simone's curves, buttocks, and thighs were revealed through her clothes. We found a café, Chez des Artistes. Glasses were clinking, the swinging doors were in constant motion, and the place was full of food.

We ordered champagne cocktails at the bar while we waited for our clothes to dry. Mademoiselle Simone laughed. "I love champagne," she said, "because it always tastes like my foot's asleep."

With affection and love,
Leon

March 6

Dear Ma:

Mademoiselle Simone hasn't been herself lately. She has shown signs of worry. This day she was as white as a sheet, she who is usually so charming, so playful.

M. Legrand and his wife, Madame Odelette, had approached Mademoiselle Simone about her marrying this French dentist, M. Vincent, with his greasy bicycle hanging from the ceiling next to his drill and his garlic breath. Mademoiselle Simone doesn't want to give up the painter's life. Her father sent her a letter which said in part, ". . . I have no further illusions about the future you hold in store for us, alas. We have had only too many occasions to experience all the ferocity, all the wicked-

ness, of your instincts for what you call fine art and your terrifying selfishness." A dentist, Ma! How do you like that?

All my love,
Leon

March 19

Dear Ma:

    Mademoiselle Simone came in to school the other day with a painting of a cheerless sky, blotted-out colors, and a mood of depression. She was wearing a squirrel coat with dried egg on the collar. On the dried egg other eggs had dried, together with dandruff, barley, bread crumbs, bobby pins, and curly hairs. Her eyes came out of the fur to look, then her nose, then her mouth, then it all went under again, then out again to shout, "I am a collage!" We all broke up laughing. She is outrageous!

    I do worry about Mademoiselle Simone. I'd be seeing her again for sure. I made affectionate gestures. I didn't know what to do. She was kissing me good-bye. Our pantomime sent the students into stitches. They imitated our kisses. Our effusions were too funny with all the alfalfa and dried eggs all over Mademoiselle Simone and myself.

    Mademoiselle Simone and I were passing through a dank section of Rue de Rivoli where there were a number of the dingiest buildings ever squeezed together. We unexpectedly spotted M. Legrand and Madame Odelette. We made a low getaway and ducked into a dark printshop nearby.

    Later, Mademoiselle Simone and I were up at Montmartre, where we discovered a brassy bar filled with noisy students and tourists. We both had some Perrier and a gâteau, after which we climbed up the steps toward the Sacré Coeur and talked about surrealism. Mademoiselle Simone had unbounded enthusiasm for the Marx Brothers, especially Harpo and his exalted expres-

175

sion. I said that Groucho without dialogue was really the best
. . . the most impossible.

From the terraced gardens near Sacré Coeur we spotted M.
Legrand and Madame Odelette coming up the steps toward us. It
seems they are actually gazing at us as if they expect a revelation.
They keep looking around, and we are aware of their advance
from step to step. They are trying to catch up to us and we decide
not to let them. We are all excited, charging around street after
street à la Jackson Pollock, scribbling down from Rue de la
Banque toward the Bourse to Avenue de l'Opéra into Rue de
Valois, turning right into Rue St. Honoré down Rue de Rivoli
and across Palais Royal into the Métro, leaving Mademoiselle
Simone for some shopping at Galeries Lafayette.

Later on in the day I took a long walk through the Bois
toward the boathouse and there was M. Legrand sitting on a
bench reading Figaro, pretending he hasn't seen me. On the way
back from the boathouse I crossed the street so as not to run into
him again, but he had followed the sun to the seat on the other
side. It was impossible to catch the son of a bitch. I was going to
grab him. The stinker was quick enough. He dashed into a clump
of trees in the Bois. I thought he was going to fly away. I shouted
after him: "A dentist to marry, is it?" He ran sideways like a
crab. A passing Frenchman slowed me down, shaking his head
as he said, "All these scenes, this ranting, this uproar without
furthering your cause . . ." Another Frenchman joined in. He
laughed and pointed at the disappearing M. Legrand, saying,
"Maître, the younger generation nowadays have murder in their
bones! Take it from me, that kind of thing will land you in the
Bastille." I let him drool; I looked away at the gardens in the
distance, the lawns, the birds hopping around the benches.

All my love,
Leon

★ ★ ★

Dear Ma:

Mademoiselle Simone didn't sell a thing at her exhibition. At the end of the month not a single buyer had appeared. In a fit of desperation she offered her entire lot of pictures stacked in her studio for the total sum of eight hundred francs, and no one availed themselves of the offer. I cheered her up saying that Van Gogh had been a peintre uniquement, *a painter and nothing but a painter. Yet there are those today who buy Van Goghs for millions each, whereas in his own time he never sold a single one.*

Madame Odelette, Mademoiselle Simone's mother, also "paints." She does pinched watercolors as a hobby and is a big hit with the relatives.

All my love,
Leon

Dear Ma:
I sent Mademoiselle Simone a poem I wrote.

>Madame Odelette
>Rococo, balloon, girlish
>At sixty
>Full of Louis Periods
>Painted the same little watercolors
>Every day
>Gave them as gifts again
>And again
>To the same people
>Until
>A stroke toppled her over, crushing
>Monsieur Legrand
>Husband, academician, classicist
>Dandy

Chevalier of the Legion of Honor
Bearded
In the manner of the day
Connoisseur
Introvert and extrovert
Worldly
Renaissance man
Flattened into a rose tracery
Sparkling
As a host of plaster cherubs
Lift them heavenward
Monsieur
Fatally pasted to Madame
Rises
Wafer thin, light shining
Through
Red, blue, violet
Stained glass.

Beauty comes back at you in the night. It attacks you. It carries you away. Although Mademoiselle Simone was undoubtedly a black sheep, her talents in paint were so obvious that it was impossible to refuse to award her art a prize and yet . . . She left, one day, with her paint box and satchel. As the train was pulling out, the distress came over her something awful. "Leon! Leon!" she hollered across the tracks over all the racket.

> *With affection and love,*
> *Leon*

A Summer with
No End

◇

May 12

I am having a difficult time with Ma. Today she says that she wants to leave the Home before the end of the week. I tell her what I heard about Mrs. Brier, who is eighty-one and still lives in Ma's old apartment building, on Undercliff Avenue, in the West Bronx. Mrs. Brier woke up one night and found a thief standing at the foot of her bed. When she sat up, he ran farther into the dark apartment. Mrs. Brier screamed and then jumped out onto the fire escape, crying for help.

Ma tells me that yesterday the Burns guards put her on the seventh floor north, in the room with the vegetable people, and then took ten dollars to bring her back out, even though Mr. Seligman, the director of the Home, has put NO TIPPING signs all over. I ask Ma what the vegetable people are like. She shudders and says, "Dreadful, Leon. The end of the line."

Ma says the Home is full of "foreigners"—stray old people who sneak in off the streets. You can't tell who is who, she says, because the illegals walk around smiling and saying "Good day" and "How do you feel?" At dinner last night, she says, there was trouble: six people at a table that seats only three. "Who to feed?" says Ma. "Some of the illegals go in and out of the kitchen, carrying trays and imitating the waiters. 'Have a little extra,' they urge. Seligman is half crazy stamping papers. The Burns guards arrest the ones who are definitely outsiders. They drive them away by car and deposit them near Webster Avenue. Seligman's son, Meyer, came up for a food check, to get us to eat less. He says bread crusts must be eaten before we touch anything else."

We walk outside into a sunny day. "The old are disappearing from hunger," Ma says.

"You're ninety-two, Ma, and you'll live forever," I tell her.

We run into Mr. Kessler, a tall octogenarian, who is feeding the birds in the little park behind the Home. He stands there covered with sparrows. His coat pockets are full of bread crumbs, and he offers them to the birds a pinch at a time.

Ma introduces us. He calls her Drezzle, her nickname from the Old Country.

"Mr. Kessler," she says, "graces our table with anecdotes and stories, entertaining us as we eat."

He returns the compliment. "Your mother possesses an unusual amount of charm. Her manner is vivacious, and her whole personality belongs to a woman of gentle birth and good breeding."

Ma smiles as we move on. "Mr. Kessler," she says, "reminds me of your father."

May 19
When I arrive at the Home today, a Burns guard tells me that Ma left her room yesterday morning and took a taxi to her old apartment on Undercliff Avenue. She tried to open the door with her key, which no longer fit, since the lock was changed three years ago. Ma was befuddled when she found a family living in the apartment. A squad car delivered her back to the Home, and her social worker took her to the infirmary, where she was given sedation.

I tell Ma that the streets in her old neighborhood in the West Bronx are deserted, that people won't go out in the middle of the day for fear of being robbed, maimed, or even murdered. But Ma misses her friends of many years and her old life. She is convinced that she has come to the Home to die.

"One limps, another shakes and coughs," she says, "this one is blind, and that one can't swallow."

At noon, I take Ma out to eat at the Pancake. The waitress, Susan, tickles her under the chin and calls her Buttercup. Ma does have a sunny look, like the late Maurice Chevalier: a fixed smile and sky-blue eyes.

Ma tells me that there was an announcement over the loudspeaker system and from now on it is forbidden to call the Home the Old Age Home. Everybody has to call it the Citizens' Rest Haven, she says. This worries her. She whispers to me that the streets are full of "outsiders"— homeless old people loaded high with bedding, waiting to sneak into the Home. The doctors here are in collusion with the Department of Health, she says, and for a fee they countersign medical certificates for the outsiders, to ensure quick entry into the Home.

"There are new arrivals from Brownsville," she says. "Everybody is getting moved up a floor. The second to the third, and the third to the fourth, and so on. A lightning count was taken Monday. Still there is the same four hundred. Leon, what happened to a whole floor of people?"

"They've joined the cavalry, Ma."

May 28

After the Friday-night service in the chapel, Rabbi Bernstein speaks: "It's the popular thing today to consider the old as 'throwaways.' Those of us in sanctuary here in the Home, off the remorseless streets, thank God for His goodness. Our brothers and sisters on the outside did not ask to be homeless. They are and will remain part of our family, and we will not rest until they are housed and taken care of. Amen."

"In Europe," Ma tells me afterward, outside the chapel, "there was a great family connectedness. A parent could become a child in all innocence, and a child could become a parent. People came together by their last name."

I embrace Ma. Her new roommate, Mrs. Landau, comes forward, puckering her lips for a kiss. I have great hope that she and Ma will be compatible. Mrs. Landau turns to Ma and says, "Drezzle, tomorrow they are going to evacuate the Home."

Ma overwhelms her with questions: "Where to? On foot? The sick as well? Those who cannot walk?"

I take Ma by the arm, and we walk to the cafeteria, in the basement. There she introduces me to two new residents, Mr. and Mrs. Stein, who smile at Ma and ask, "How do you feel?" Ma tells me that they were outsiders who brought letters of recommendation from a Brooklyn congressman. "Now," she says, "dozens of outsiders are coming in their underwear with recommendations from God knows who."

When Ma and I go up to the lobby, Mr. Kessler is there, surrounded by a group of people. He breaks away to greet us. He is dressed in a sports jacket, a plaid shirt, and a bow tie.

"It's the new style," he says, seizing both Ma's hands and shaking them heartily. "Drezzle, you don't feel disposed to take a brisk walk over to Fordham Road? I know a steak house where we can have a red-hot chop for dinner and a glass of good wine."

Ma excuses herself graciously, saying, "Another time, maybe."

June 19

"The Burns guards," Ma tells me, "bored holes in the back wall. They pass large amounts of food through the holes to Seligman's son, Meyer, who comes in a pickup truck. When they catch sight of Seligman himself, they shout a warning, and Meyer drives off. Later, he sells the food back to Seligman at twice the price."

Ma leans forward and lowers her voice. "The illegals are demanding clothing from everybody. At the least sign of opposition, they threaten to go to Seligman. Frightening, if true, since Seligman could turn on the legitimates and throw us out of the Home. Some of the illegals also had their names changed for a price. After three or four changes, they got their original names back again."

We are walking in the corridor, and Ma looks around to

make sure we are not overheard. She tells me that one of the waiters beat Mr. Resnick over the head with a tray at two o'clock in the morning, shouting, "You have diamonds! Where are they hidden?"

When we get back to the room, Mrs. Landau, Ma's roommate, is watching "All in the Family." She turns to tell us about a rumor that the Home is serving horsemeat for dinner.

"The mood here is very bad," says Ma. "Seligman grows restless. The social workers say he is going to sell the Home to the government for a highway project."

Ma went to the beauty parlor this morning. She had a mudpack on her face and a henna rinse, and she looks very strange with orange hair. We run into Mr. Kessler, and he does not seem to notice any difference in her appearance. On leaving, he shakes hands with her and says, "Pray you, madame, remain as you are."

June 23
The weather is sunny, and the elderly from the Home are out in front, packing the sidewalk behind the gates, opening and closing their folding chairs. It is a windy day, and they have to sit quickly once their chairs are open. One woman is caught in a gust and plunges into a hedge. The old people settle in, cranelike, grumbling about the tight fit and the changing neighborhood. Ma is at her window, and I wave to her as I approach the Home.

When I enter her room, Ma complains that the night nurse ordered her to dance on one leg for bed-wetting. Ma had been hiding bread on a high shelf in the closet, but the nurse miraculously climbed up and ate it. "What are we to do?" Ma moans, pressing her hands to her cheeks. "Are we to dole out bread to everyone and anyone?"

Ma confides that she found Mrs. Kroll from Lafontaine Avenue in bed next to her last night. "It's not the first time. I'm not even sure that it's Mrs. Kroll every night. I never see her, but I know her back and her feet. She wraps herself in my blanket and shoves me. I push her with my knees. I take hold of her ankles and place them far over, to get her feet out of my face. My sleep is very light, and now I am awake and now I am asleep."

I help Ma to get ready for a stroll on the terrace. She puts on a hat with a wide brim and a gauze veil for protection from the sun. I hadn't realized how tiny and thin she has become. I have to pull up her stockings five times on our way to the terrace.

We pass a large woman in an Empress Eugénie hat and a flared coat trimmed with monkey fur. "That's Mrs. Gelb," says Ma. "She's been here a whole year without discovery. She was carried in through a side entrance for a price. Once inside, she was on her own." Ma points to a group of old women sitting on chairs on the terrace, facing away from each other. "They are here since 1954, on special papers, and are allowed to remain. Those who are still on the street are eating out of garbage cans."

June 25

"Last night was terrible," Ma says, shaking her head. "They threw Resnick out of the window along with his chair."

I ask her who Resnick is, and she doesn't know.

"Today," she says, "was worse than yesterday. A group from Flatbush arrived in a truck. Ten had broken limbs from the ride. Seligman wept at the sight and received them with coffee and cake. Everybody is giving them presents."

At the Friday-night service, Rabbi Bernstein speaks of the sorrowful condition of the old and says that all elderly poor should be eligible for food and shelter. During his sermon, Ma whispers to me that the social workers say Rabbi Bernstein is looking for trouble with his "everybody is equal" routine.

Ma is upset tonight. Back in her room, she points out the window to a brick wall that is under construction. I explain that they are enlarging the Home to add another three hundred beds for some of the destitute old people trying to get in. But Ma is convinced that the brick wall means something awful. "Leon, they say Seligman is poisoning the soup to speed us up and make way for the outsiders."

Mrs. Landau comes in. She turns on the TV with a firm hand. "Life goes on, Drezzle," she says. "The Burns guards are on duty, postmen deliver the mail, newspapers come out daily, telephone services continue, garbage is collected. This will be a summer with no end." Ma has stopped listening to her.

July 7

When I see Ma today, she is wearing Mrs. Landau's teeth, which are too large for her gums and give her a strangely stern appearance. With one hand to her mouth, Ma says that more Burns guards have been hired and that they make daily raids on the increasing number of illegals. "This morning, Leon!" she says. "Barricades everywhere! Exits blocked! A fruitless chase—the illegals hid in the basement."

Ma is afraid that if she complains about her health or looks sickly, she will be killed outright.

We pass by the leathercraft room on the third floor

south. A number of women are in there, cutting, weaving, gluing, sewing. The room is a mess of chopped and tangled pigskin leftovers.

"From morning to night they're making leather clubs and whips," says Ma.

There are a lot of faces to kiss at the Home today. There's Rosie, an old friend of Ma's, to kiss, and some new ones—Sylvia, Mary, and Lilly. I kiss a Mrs. Harris, a woman in her eighties, with a large pink face, who has come up sighing about old times: "When we were all considerate of each other's feelings sitting down to a meal. When handing food to a neighbor was of greater importance than eating ourselves."

After Ma and I are alone again, she says, "You forgot to kiss Seligman and the Burns guards."

July 10

Ma is in bed again today. She hardly recognizes me at first. When she is sure it's me, she says, "Some of the social workers are supplying the illegals with clothing and linen and a little money to get started again, but somewhere else. Only last Sunday, outsiders from the Grand Concourse were received very warmly by Seligman and a committee of social workers. But then the next day five busloads arrived from Brooklyn. Three hundred and fifty—all were turned away. Burns guards were shoving them back into the buses. Leon, the sight was unforgettable. In the end, the poor will be without a place to lay their heads."

My brother Ronald arrives at the Home in a blue serge suit, a white shirt with a button-down collar, and a black tie. His wife, Doris, wears a tan gabardine suit and a pink kettle-shaped hat, which give her a safari appearance.

"I am a woman over ninety, Hazel," Ma tells her. "So many women wander into self-doubt at a much earlier age, but I took good care of myself."

Ma has Doris mixed up with Ronald's first wife, Hazel, and Ronald is upset. "It's Doris, Ma, Doris, not Hazel, Ma, Doris."

"Hazel, I used to put Ronald's shoes and pants on until he was twelve years old."

July 14

Ma is all set for running away today. Some load she has ready: a satchel, bedding, pocketbooks, and, on top, pictures of the whole family from forty years ago. The stuff clanks every time she tries to lift it. She says she is fed up looking at old people. "The outsiders stand near the front entrance and wait for someone to have pity on them. You look out the window and see faces. Some are lying down because they are too weak to stand. Some of them sing in the courtyard. They are hoping for tossed coins. At night, Leon—the cries of the hungry! Seligman walks around in boots and talks like a dictator. He says that the dollar is falling and soon we'll have to pay in foreign currency. Some of the Burns guards dress in civilian clothes and lounge around in the lobby. Then suddenly they dash into the dining room and seize people sitting down to a meal and throw them out on the street."

I assure Ma that she is ten times safer in the Home than out of it. I read her a headline from the *News:* "ELDERLY BRONX WOMAN FLEES MUGGER, BREAKS BOTH LEGS."

July 21

Mrs. Landau had a stroke on Sunday and is in the infirmary. When I go up to see her, she is fighting for breath.

Her face is yellow and covered with sweat, like a wax mask beginning to melt. She wants to tell me something, but she can't.

Ma has told me that Mr. Kessler is now seen walking around with Mrs. Klingman, who used to be a high-class tailor and is putting suits together for him. Today they promenade past us in the lobby. Mr. Kessler is in possession of a jacket, trousers, and gloves of rough fabric in striking colors. Mrs. Klingman is heavy with jewelry, and has given herself a complete overhauling: dyed black hair, powder and rouge, and violet eyelids. Ma shrugs and says, "Hers is the triumph of the woman of eighty when she lets herself loose, may she burn!"

Ma remains sitting in her room this afternoon—bent and thin, her head drooping.

"At the end of the world, when the ram's horn is blown, they'll turn into mice," she says. When I don't ask who, she continues. "There is a new decree. Women may not have hairdos or wear high heels or slacks. But there are those whom Seligman favors. These people live in luxury—all others may perish. Everywhere you turn, there are beggars. A large group arrived from Hunts Point this morning, looking for an opportunity to smuggle themselves in."

July 28

Mrs. Landau died on Monday, and Ma has a new roommate, Mrs. Benson. She is a stout woman in a wheelchair. Her hands are muffled in mittens to prevent thumb-sucking, and because of some impediment she cannot speak. Her pale-gray eyes beam with a steady benevolence that is not put into words.

I get permission to take Ma to the Pancake. She has

become incontinent, so her Chinese nurse, Miss Ling, takes her to the john and diapers her with a large sheet. Ma doesn't like the handling she gets, and she calls my sister's name. "Marion! Marion!" she cries in a hoarse voice. "Help me!" Marion is in Miami and doesn't hear her. I reassure Ma that she'll feel better once we get out. This may be the last time she will be able to leave the Home.

One of the relatives visited Ma yesterday, and "Drezzle's sinking fast" went over the telephone lines to members of the family. Tonight the calls come from all over. Uncle Sidney phones to say what a marvel Ma was in the old days: "Roses in her cheeks, Leon. As you know, she's my favorite girl in the whole family." Aunt Harriet phones: "Leon, it was only last week I spoke to Drezzle." My sister Marion phones from Miami. "I hear that Ma is sinking fast," she says. I reassure her: "Ma walked around the Home three times with me this afternoon. She's young in spirit, with all her moles, wrinkles, and whiskers. Ma is fine. Really, Marion."

August 4
Today I find Ma in bed, napping. "Arise!" I shout. "It's the dawn of a new day!"

She is annoyed by my sudden arrival. "Ah, reptile," she says, "I often wonder who you take after. Certainly not your father or me." Then she shifts to an intimate tone of voice to tell me that Seligman's son, Meyer, removed the silverware from the dining room and that at dinner last night she had to pluck at the steaming potatoes with her fingers. She says that she went down to talk to Seligman about this but was told that the director does not talk to the residents, as a matter of principle.

Ma tells me that the elderly who crowd the street outside the Home this week are very polite. "They say 'Ladies and gentlemen, may we have something to eat?' and 'Thank you' and 'God bless.' If they didn't stick out their hands, Leon, you would never guess they were beggars. Everyone looks after themselves first and foremost. I am afraid to walk outside the room. And when we go to eat, we march in rows of six. Speaking is forbidden."

There is a suffocating smell in Ma's room, and when I leave the Home I rush into the open air.

August 8
Ma has been moved into the infirmary. She doesn't recognize me, and calls me Ronald—my brother's name.

A bell rings, and as if at a command signal most of the old people in the infirmary speak at once. Amid the clamor of voices, each of which is raised louder and louder, Ma and I cry out to hear one another. After a few minutes of such exercise, Ma is voiceless, and we are compelled simply to sit without speaking. Such a visit is torture.

August 18
Ma has been moved into the infirmary again. Her face is black and blue from a fall she took the day before yesterday. "The social workers are letting outsiders into the Home in batches," she tells me. "They let in one batch, wait a moment, let in another batch, counting them off, mostly in groups of twelve. Seligman is issuing meal tickets. He's giving orders at the entrance. A striking figure. From a social worker the outsiders get a splash of

soup each. They sit down on the sidewalk and slurp it, smack their lips, poke one another, and spill soup all over. Some clap their hands in wonder and say 'God bless.' But what about us? The mood in the Home is very bad. It is only Wednesday, and the food for the week is already eaten. Seligman sent the social workers on food missions to buy on credit."

Ma is white as a sheet and is all upset. She looks as if she hasn't slept.

"The illegals keep getting in, more of them every day. And the crowd outside . . . I see people fall. One woman gets up with a cry, the others lie where they are. The mob presses over them, treading on them. They scream for food. They're crazy! At least a hundred of them. . . . Seligman is out like a shot to speak the truth. 'Make way! Make way!' He pushes through the crowd. 'I have no illusions about the future,' he shouts. 'We here in the Home know only too well the wickedness of your instincts for eating, your terrifying appetites. We have done our best, tried everything, now we are at the end of our rope. We ourselves are out of food. Now you must count on yourselves alone. Count on us no longer, we beg of you. The Home and I are at the end of our patience. There is nothing more to eat.' Nobody moves. Poor Seligman shrieks at the top of his lungs that there is no food and no shelter.

"They get Seligman from behind. He is still resisting. . . . It's shameful. Even so, he throws kisses to those of us watching from the windows of the Home. We understand him. The outsiders push and shove and bark like dogs. . . . Seligman is waving his arms, working himself up into a frenzy. He is going to say something. His words sound tortured. . . . It's unbelievable. The Burns guards have come out, laughing. They are turned loose on the mob. They grab the ones that are shouting the loudest. The horde breaks down the gates, bending the bars, ripping them out of the cement. They storm the door, they flood into the entrance, they move about on all fours. . . . I feel them coming, pressing up against the glass doors of the lobby, a pack of old faces. . . ."